JERO

D1649357

PRAISE FOR
JEROME DOOLITTLE'S
<u>STRANGLE HOLD</u>

Books by Jerome Doolittle

Body Scissors
Strangle Hold
Bear Hug

Published by POCKET BOOKS

JEROME DOOLITTLE

BEAR HUG

A TOM BETHANY MYSTERY

POCKET BOOKS

New York   London   Toronto   Sydney   Tokyo   Singapore

This book is a work of fiction. Names, characters, places and incidents are either products of the author's imagination or are used fictitiously. Any resemblance to actual events or locales or persons, living or dead, is entirely coincidental.

POCKET BOOKS, a division of Simon & Schuster Inc.
1230 Avenue of the Americas, New York, NY 10020

ISBN: 0-671-74569-7

First Pocket Books paperback printing November 1993

10 9 8 7 6 5 4 3 2 1

POCKET and colophon are registered trademarks of Simon & Schuster Inc.

Cover art by Robert Grace

Printed in the U.S.A.

TO CONNIE

1

IT WAS WHAT WOULD HAVE been the mud season up in the Champlain Valley, that time when winter hasn't gone out yet and spring hasn't come in yet. The farm machinery has long since been repaired and is all ready to go, but you still can't get in the ground to plant, and it looks like winter is never going to end. There's not a damned thing to do but kick the dog or whip your son or rape your daughter or beat your wife, or just shoot yourself and all of the above to death, and the final hell with everything.

Mud season is the biggest reason why the principal export of Port Henry, New York, is human beings. Every mud season I'm glad all over again that I joined the crowd as soon as I was old enough to enlist in the army. The army shipped me off to Laos, which was a lot of things, some good and some bad and some muddy. But even when it was muddy, it wasn't mud season.

It was never really mud season in Cambridge, either,

even if there had been a certain amount of freezing and thawing in the February just ending. For the real thing you need a long, deep winter to freeze your brain solid right through. That way it cracks to pieces when the thaws come and go, just like the roads in the north country do. Cambridge is too near the sea for that kind of weather, too far south.

Still, it was pretty lousy out. At seven-thirty the sun may have been up there somewhere, but it wasn't getting through the clouds. The snow had melted, exposing all the street crud built up over the last two or three months. Whenever the weather got around to drying up, the litter would start to blow around and call attention to itself. For the moment, though, it was plastered onto the wet pavement like just another part of it. Cold rain had been gusting on and off all night.

But what did I care? I was dry as a bone, thanks to the Australian stockman's coat I was draping over the stool next to mine in The Tasty. Joey Neary hadn't turned away from the grill when I walked in, but he must have seen me out of the corner of his eye. "Nice-looking coat, Bethany," he said. "I think I'll get one for my pony."

"Take this one, do you good. You look a little low."

"Let me tell you about low. I'm coming up on the end of a midnight-to-eight, I'm naturally feeling like a used douche bag, and then this asshole comes in with some kind of Paul Hogan coat on and he's looking happy as a pig in shit."

"I am happy, Joey. I was up at six, I did my stretches, I went down to the river and ran my four miles, never mind the rain and the mud and the cold. You have any idea how superior that makes me feel? To you, for example? What I'm telling you here, Joey, I'm feeling really good about myself. I'm number one again."

"Know what I'm telling you, Bethany? Just two words. *Fuck* and *you*."

"Yeah, well, I also got two for you. *Ham* and eggs."

I had grabbed a *Globe* at the Out-of-Town Newsstand across Mass. Ave., and I glanced at the front page while Joey cracked the eggs and sliced the ham. Slow news day. A couple of murders in Roxbury, and something about the wonders of smart bombs. As near as I could make out, George Bush was using these smart bombs as a meat extender. His meat.

"Take a look at this," I said when Joey had my breakfast popping in the grease. He wiped his hands on his apron and took the card I held out. He looked at it and then checked the photo against me.

"I don't get it," he said. "How come the card says Henderson and it's got your picture on it?"

"I lied."

"You're working for the *Globe* now?"

"No, of course not. I got my pride."

"So how come you got a press card?"

"I made it."

"But the thing's laminated and all."

"I got it laminated, Joey. What can I say?"

"What do you mean, you made it?"

"On my computer. A person I got involved with a little while back, he died and left me all his software. Part of it was a program to make certificates and stuff."

"How come you made a press card?"

"I made all kinds of shit. I got one says I'm special assistant to the president of Harvard. One says I'm an investigator for the Addison County attorney's office."

"Where's Addison County?"

"In New Jersey, according to my card."

"How do you know what a *Boston Globe* card looks like?"

"Doesn't everybody know?"

"How would anybody know?"

"Exactly."

Joey thought about that for a moment and nodded. "I get your point," he said. He turned back to the grill and rescued my breakfast before it could frizzle away to nothing. He loaded a plate, garnished it with Wonder Bread toasted on one side, and slid it in front of me. "What I don't get is the whole point," he said. "Why do you want a bunch of phony cards?"

"Helps me pick up girls."

"No, seriously."

"Seriously, I don't really know. I got a computer, I'm just fucking around with it. See what I can do."

"Well, seeing as we're talking seriously, Tom," Joey said, and stopped for a moment, embarrassed. The "Tom" made me know he was serious, for a fact. In our usual back-and-forth, I was always Bethany. "I don't know what you do, actually," he finally went on. "None of my fucking business, right? Only the idea I got is you find things out, look into things for people. Don't tell me if I'm wrong or I'm right. Just tell me if you could help out a bunch of old guys I know, that they want to find out something."

"Old guys?"

"One of them's my uncle Kevin, comes in here sometimes. You seen him. One leg."

"Didn't know he was your uncle."

"Well, he don't talk much. Anyway, him and these other old guys, they can pay. A little something, anyway."

"What's their problem?"

"They were all in this kind of investment club, and they got fucked out of their money."

"Who by?"

"Some guy down in Houston. This dead guy."

4

A Harvard kid came in just then, up early for Harvard kids. In with him came a sudden slug of wind, cold, and damp. Rain rattled like shot on the plate-glass window. "I was in basic with a bubba from Houston," I told Joey. "According to what this bubba said, they only got two seasons down there. February and summer."

Back when I was working for Teddy Kennedy in Iowa I was listed as security and as his pilot. But in addition to being a flying bodyguard, I was a gofer and a rememberer, too. One of the main things I had to remember was names. I'd do it the old-fashioned way, by association. He's kind of short, and his name is Thompson, so Tom Thumb. He's also the mayor and his first name is Harry, and Clint Eastwood was a mayor, so Dirty Harry Tom Thumb. I don't know why this works, since it means remembering more instead of less, but it seems to. Maybe because I have practically a photographic memory anyway, at least for written stuff.

So when Joey Neary introduced me a couple of days later to his uncle Kevin and four other old-timers, I repeated the names after each introduction and made up my little stories. Ed Cleary was Ed the egg, clearly bald. And so on. Moving right along, then, the three others were Chris Costello, Brian Mooney, and Marty Maginnis. All of them looked to be in their late sixties or their seventies. Maginnis could even have been in his eighties. I don't know whether seniority still counts when everybody's got so much of it, but Maginnis was the group's talker.

"Could you use a little something, Tom?" he asked. "The bar don't open for an hour yet, but the bartender is my nephew."

"Maybe after a while," I said. "Why don't we get the business over first?"

"Well, let's sit then. Bethany. Is that Irish?"

"I don't think so."

"I thought not. I never heard of it as being Irish."

"Tell you the truth, I never looked into it," I said, which was almost true. But I did know that Bethany was a town where Jesus had his men steal a horse for him. Maybe the name was Jewish, for all I knew. Jesus was.

"There's plenty of Catholics aren't Irish," the old man said.

"I'm not one of them. My mother went to the Witness Hall for a while, till the old man found out she was giving them money. The old man himself was too busy for church. He spent Sundays drunk, same as every other day."

"Sounds to me like he had Irish blood," Joey Neary said.

"Joey," said his uncle, scolding.

"Well, shit, I bring you a guy that maybe can help you out, the point isn't what parish he belongs to."

"Marty was just making talk."

"That's true," Marty Maginnis said. "But the boy's right, too. We can get acquainted after we do our business."

We were sitting around a poker table covered in green baize that was coming unglued in one corner. In the center was an ashtray made out of the base of a 155-millimeter artillery shell. It was piled high with cigarette butts. Although the poker chips had been put away somewhere, nothing else had been cleaned up from whenever the last game had been. We were just off Central Square, not far from police headquarters, but the chances were zero that Cambridge cops would ever knock over a friendly game in the Francis X. Sullivan Post of the American Legion. Maginnis set the ashtray on the floor, took a stab at blowing the tabletop clean, and set a thick manila envelope on it.

"Your mission, should you choose to accept it," Joey said.

"This here is all the paperwork," Maginnis said. "Let me fill you in on the background."

It was another one of those Morning-in-America stories. The old-timers, along with a half-dozen or so others who hadn't been able to make it to the meeting, were World War II vets. "It's my fault, I'm ashamed to say," Maginnis said, and everybody else jumped in to say it wasn't his fault at all.

"Still, it was," he insisted. "I was the one doing so damned well for myself, and I was the one that got all you fellows on board."

Maginnis's daughter was married to a man who knew a man who knew all about making money grow through the magic of junk bonds and government-insured deposits in a Texas savings and loan that paid interest you wouldn't believe. And shouldn't have, as it turned out.

"We got together in kind of an investment club with this fellow, Mortenson was his name, handling things for us. Doesn't dare show his face around anymore, he doesn't. Down in Florida, from what I understand. He should be someplace where it's a good deal hotter than that. Thanks to him, we lost every penny."

"I thought you said it was government insured."

"Oh, that's what we thought, all right. What we was led to believe. What we find out is something different, though. At first we had it in this Sunbanc Savings and Loan, down there in Houston, and that was all right. That was insured by the FDIC, just like Mortenson said. But behind Sunbanc was this doctor named Somerville, like Somerville the town. Denton Somerville."

"Oh, shit," I said. I hadn't kept track of every single

piece of pond scum that floated to the top of the business pages during the supply-side years, but anyone reading the papers a couple of years ago couldn't miss Somerville's name. Dr. Denton they called him, naturally.

"This Somerville, Mortenson was working for him is what it amounted to. What they did was get suckers to take their money out of Sunbanc and put it into bonds of the holding company that owned Sunbanc. Suckers like us. Mortenson told us that the bonds were insured, same as the S and L deposits were."

"Tell you in writing?" I asked, gesturing at the thick manila envelope.

"No, he just told us personally. He was our financial adviser."

"Our friend," put in Chris Costello, same initials as Chris Columbus. "You got that prick for a friend, you don't need an enemy."

"How much money we talking about here?" I asked.

"All of it," Maginnis said. "When the S and L went belly up, those bonds weren't worth a cent. Between us, the whole club, we lost just short of three hundred thousand dollars."

"Holy shit."

"Yeah, I know what you're thinking. You're thinking here's a bunch of guys on Social Security playing nickeldime poker down at the Legion Hall, where do they come up with that kind of money?"

Since that was exactly what I was thinking, I didn't say anything. And Maginnis went on.

"The thing is, all of us worked straight through till retirement. Not big money jobs, not by no means. Motorman, MTA dispatcher, bartender, maintenance engineer, like that. But steady. You never get rich, but like Howie Mortenson showed us, you build up equity. You got your house maybe, or most of it. An insurance policy with cash value. Maybe money you can take out of your retirement, a lump sum."

"Oh, no," I said. Howie was a nice piece of work.

"Yeah," Maginnis said. "That's what Ed here done. He took it out of his union retirement, much as he could, and now his monthly check's down to twenty-eight bucks. That right, Ed? Twenty-eight."

"Twenty-seven fifty-two, you want to be exactly right."

"One of the guys that couldn't come tonight, he done practically the same thing. Anyway, Mortenson was right. You take a dozen dumb fucks like us that think they don't have a pot to piss in, show 'em how to do it, you'd be surprised how much they can come up with. By the way, that's what we used to call our little invest-ment club, the Diamond Dozen. Like dime-a-dozen, you know? Only like diamond ring, too, that kind of dia-mond. Now we call ourselves the Dummy Dozen."

"Three hundred thousand, it comes out to twenty-five each," I said.

"Some more, some less."

"Was anybody really wiped out?"

"Like sleeping down the Pine Street shelter? No, not that bad. Mortenson couldn't figure out any way for us to get at our Social Security and city pensions. And you always got the family behind you. But it hurts, that does. All your life they been counting on you, now it's the other way around."

"And you got no cushion," Chris Costello said. "Look at us, jeez, any of us could have to go into the nursing home tomorrow."

"My favorite granddaughter got married three weeks ago," Cleary said, "which normally you couldn't have kept me away from. But Tucson? What was I going to do, borrow the airfare from her parents that just got through paying for the wedding? I told them the doctor said I couldn't fly."

"A lot of us took out mortgages we can't pay off," Maginnis said. "I'm looking at probably losing my home, same way with four or five others of us. You figure you finally made it to harbor and all of a sudden you're way out at sea again."

"What do you think I could do?" I asked. "This Dr. Denton died a while back, didn't I read in the papers?"

"Died of a heart attack, yes. While he was out on bail."

"Right. And you tell me this guy Mortenson is in Florida, which I understand is where assholes like him move to, because state law won't let the creditors attach your house there, no matter how big it is."

"Mortenson got screwed himself," Maginnis said. "He bought the same bonds he sold us, and went down with his own ship. I heard he was working in an auto parts store in Fort Myers."

"So what's left?"

"That's what we were hoping you could find out. Look, on the news they said that son of a bitch Somerville, his S and L had assets of two billion dollars. Not million. *Billion*. That much money don't just disappear, does it? Some of it must still be lying around down there somewhere."

"And you think I could get hold of it?"

"That I wouldn't know. I was just talking to Joey one day and he said he knew this guy came into the coffee shop and why not see what he says? That's all we're doing here, we're just reaching for straws."

"You hear that, Bethany?" Joey said. "You're a straw."

"That ain't what he meant, Joey," Kevin said. "If you wasn't Mary's boy, I'd have to say you was a major pain in the ass sometimes."

"You hear that, Joey?" I said. "You're a pain in the ass."

And then to Maginnis: "And I'm a straw, no doubt about that. I think all you got here is straws, though. I doubt anybody can do anything. You got screwed is all, just like millions of other people that voted for the actor."

I reached for the fat manila envelope. "Let me look at what you got anyway, all right? Just in case. And I'll poke around in the library for a couple of days, see what I come up with. Which let me warn you right now, it's not liable to be anything."

"All we can ask," Maginnis said. "Now that's out of the way, at least we can buy a drink for you, can't we?"

"At least."

I spent happy hour in the Legion bar with the five members of the Dummy Dozen, and then went home to look through the manila envelope. It held the records of the club's dealings with Howie Mortenson, who had worked for a formerly high-riding bucket shop called Axel, Shearman. I knew from the newspapers that the firm had declared bankruptcy a couple of years ago, after all the principal thieves voted themselves millions of dollars in bonuses. Mortenson wasn't one of them. He seemed to have been just a low-level Munchkin in the Boston office, and no doubt he believed that the shit he peddled really was chocolate ice cream. At least he had eaten it himself, according to what Maginnis had said.

The envelope also held narrative accounts from each of the twelve retirees. These were mostly handwritten, although a couple were typed. Maginnis had evidently got each person to set down his memories of how, why, and where he had raised the money that went south.

Mortenson had acted as a financial planner for the men, advising them to do things like take out second mortgages so they could pay off their high-interest loans, mostly automobile and credit cards, with the lower-interest mortgage money. While they were at it, they might as well borrow right up to the limit of their home equity, put the money in Sunbanc S&L at 19 percent, pay off the 13-percent mortgage with that, and reinvest the 6-percent difference with Sunbanc, where it would, etc., etc. It all sounded pretty plausible, but so does a chain letter. I wondered how many other people Mortenson had ruined with his perpetual money machine. Probably plenty, since he was so good at it that Sunbanc wound up hiring him away from Axel, Shearman. His new job had been to sell his old customers on converting all those insured S & L accounts supported by the tax-payer into uninsured bonds supported by nothing but Sunbanc's mountain of crooked appraisals, cooked books, uncollectible loans, and unsold condos. After the collapse, those bonds became known in the business pages as Dr. Dentons, after the underwear of the same name that little kids used to wear. And after Dr. Denton Somerville. I remembered seeing his picture in the paper at the time of his death, a file photo that showed him coming out of some courthouse or other, wearing a deco-rative wife on his arm.

Next day I went off to Widener Library to find that picture again, along with whatever else I could dig up on the doctor and his multibillion-dollar scam. There was plenty. I spent the morning and early afternoon in the government documents section, where Harvard keeps its microfilmed newspaper files.

The best of the stuff on Dr. Somerville's gigantic scam was in *The Wall Street Journal*, which has a weirdly split personality. The editorial pages are in the hands of corporate flacks, neo-cons, neo-libs, Chicago economists, and similar forms of sucking life. But the news columns have been infiltrated by reporters, who can come up with some pretty good stuff. One of those reporters had had the good idea of following the money trail backward, to see where Sunbanc's billions had come from. The stories she had dug up were much worse than the ones my Dummy Dozen had to tell.

Her most unforgettable character was one *Reader's Digest* isn't ever likely to pick up on, a San Diego woman she called Sally M. Sally had been married to the owner of a sportswear store. The first she knew he was bisexual was when he told her he had AIDS. Six months later, fading fast, he sold off his business for $650,000 and put it all into various conservative investments. Then, to keep his wife's inheritance out of the hands of the doctors, he put a bullet through his brain while he still had the judgment and the strength to do it. His pregnant widow, at least, had tested free of the AIDS virus; she and the baby would be healthy and secure.

Three months after her husband's death, Sally gave birth to a baby girl. The infant had Down's syndrome. When the bills for the child's care started to mount up, Sally M. needed more income than her conservative investments brought her. The nice man with the Sunbanc Savings and Loan bonds was anxious to help. Why not? He got an 8.5-percent fee on the initial sale, plus additional "sales charges" each time the dividends were reinvested. This came to good money, too, since annual dividends were 15 percent. Meanwhile, although nobody made a big point of this to Sally M., the bonds themselves lost almost half their value in the first year she had them. She would have been surprised. The nice man had never said anything to her about junk bonds. He called them double-C bonds, which sounded to her like they must be twice as good as something or other.

And when Somerville's Ponzi scheme collapsed completely, of course, what they turned out to be twice as good as was Confederate money.

Sally wound up homeless and alcoholic, living under a bridge. She had lost her child first to the state and then to pneumonia, which killed the baby at the age of two in the pediatric intensive care unit of a San Diego hospital. No one at the hospital knew how to find Sally. But the police found her six weeks later, when she herself had been dead two days, also from pneumonia. In the packing crate where she had lived and died, the patrolmen found dozens of letters to Dr. Denton Somerville. The first letter had been written the day after she lost her home. The last one was dated three days before police found her body. She had never mailed any of them.

"Oh please oh please," the last letter ended, "make it so my baby and me can live together again so we can give each other the love every human being needs. You are a doctor, have mercy."

Reading Sally's story made me want to believe in the devil. But Somerville was no doubt rotting away just as peaceably and painlessly as if he had been Mother Teresa.

By now my eyes were blurring from hours of spooling microfilm in front of them in a darkened room. To let them recover, I went across the street for a cheeseburger at Bartley's. Then I went back across Mass. Ave. to give my eyes more punishment, this time in the periodical reading room of Widener. When the library closed, I was forced out again into the cold rain that had been falling all day. It was the end of February, pretty nearly summertime in Houston.

What I wanted to do was go down to Malkin Athletic Center, which I get to use because I help coach Harvard's wrestling team, and sweat myself limp in the team's sauna. But there wasn't enough time before closing, and so I did the second best thing. I picked up a six-pack of India Pale Ale at the L'il Peach around the corner from my apartment, went back home, opened one, sat back in my recliner, and closed my eyes in hopes they might stop burning sooner or later.

And I thought about the late Dr. Denton Somerville, and I listened to the rain hitting the window. The window leaked around the edges. In weather like this, a little stream of cold, damp air ran along the floor and out under the door to the hallway. I knew because my feet used to be always cold in the winter, before I bought my La-Z-Boy and hoisted them up out of the draft.

I was due to see the Dummy Dozen, this time all of them, at the Legion Hall tomorrow afternoon. I didn't have anything encouraging to tell them.

"It's not like there's a big pile of the stuff down in Houston if we could only find it," I said. We were back in the Legion Hall. "It isn't even real money. It never was. It was just electrons going back and forth over phone lines."

"Whatever it was, you could spend it," said old Brian Mooney. "That son of a bitch Dr. Denton, he spent it."

"He could spend it as long as he could make people believe he had it," I explained, not really understanding my own explanation. "Like Donald Trump."

"Trump's still spending it, ain't he?" Mooney said. "All I know is it was real money when I had it. How come it turned to something else? Look, that Somerville son of a bitch, he couldn't possibly have spent all that money before he died. No man alive could have. There was just too goddamned much of it. So it's got to be

15

somewhere. That's all we want to know. Where is it, and can we get any of it back?''

"I'm no expert," I said, which was the truth. All I knew was what I had plowed through in the library the day before. "But my guess is he moved a lot of it off-shore, put a lot of it in his wife's name. A lot of it the government grabbed and sold cheap to other thieves. The lawyers got a lot of it. Hell, I don't know.''

"Can you find out?''

I didn't know that, either, but I did know there had to be people in Washington who knew about hiding assets. And Washington was on the way to Houston. Even more important, it was where Hope Edwards lived. It was also where her husband lived, but Hope and I had coexisted with that problem for a long time. Just as she and Martin Edwards had coexisted with the problem that he was a first-class father to their three children, a kind, intelligent, prosperous, humorous, handsome husband—and a man who had discovered after he was married and a father that he was irrevocably homosexual.

"Tell you what," I said to Brian Mooney and the eleven other victims. "I could go down to Washington for a few days. Ask around, maybe find an IRS guy or a federal prosecutor who knows about these things. Then go down to Houston and poke around a little.''

"What would you charge to do that?" Maginnis said.

"I was going down to D.C. anyway, so you get a free ride that far. Houston I'd have to charge you. Only the thing is, you haven't got any money." I was hoping this would put an end to it. No human being ever gets his money back from dead thieves. Even governments have trouble, as the Philippines are finding out.

"We've got a little. One or two of us had enough sense to keep a few dollars where they belonged. We could pay expenses anyway, or maybe we could. Would expenses be pretty high, you think?"

"Not the way I travel, no. Four or five hundred maybe, unless I had to stay a long time."

"Well, I guess we could handle that, couldn't we, boys?"

Everybody made the right noises to that. We were in the Legion's card room again.

"I don't know," Ed Cleary said. "Doesn't seem fair to me."

"What doesn't, Ed?" Maginnis said.

"Man's got to make a living. Can't do that off of expenses."

"I'd be taking it on as a gamble," I said. "Contingency basis, like the lawyers. Whatever I get back for you, I'll take five percent."

"That's not enough," Marty Maginnis said. "The lawyers get a third, don't they?"

"Sometimes a half."

"Well, there you are. It's not enough."

"That's my final offer," I said. "Five percent, take it or leave it."

So they took it. What choice did they have? And what difference did it make, anyway? Five percent or fifty percent of nothing, it all comes to the same thing.

"Understand something," I said before we broke up. "I'll poke around down there till I'm sure it's hopeless, and then I'll come home. Realistically, that's all that's going to happen. So at the end you'll be out a few hundred bucks, with absolutely zip to show for it. Is it a deal?"

"What about it, boys?" Maginnis asked. "Is it a deal?"

And they all said it was. No wonder Mortenson had been able to skin them alive.

2

THE TABARD INN IS IN WHAT used to be a large town house on N Street, off Dupont Circle where Washington's half-dozen or so flower children used to sing antiwar songs in the long, long ago. The inn is owned by Edward Cohen and his wife, Fritzi. Edward used to be a newspaperman, also in the long, long ago. A lot of good people are ex-newspapermen, I've noticed, which probably tells you something about the business.

Edward and Fritzi had the sense to leave the old town house's big lounge pretty much the way it must have been at the turn of the century or whenever the place was last a private home. There were old Persian rugs on the floor, what I guess you'd have to call Iranian rugs nowadays. There were old prints and oil paintings on the walls, books in the bookcases, and a fat Buddha sitting on a radiator. Victorian and Empire couches and armchairs were stuck around anywhere they fit, just like in a real living room. There was no TV. Over the fireplace was a wood carving of a double eaglet painted in black and gold, the stern board off some long-gone boat. A fire burned in the fireplace when the weather was cold, which it was at the moment. The last day of February was chilly, overcast, and rainy. Umbrellas and raincoats dripped in the entrance hallway.

Hope Edwards came in, hatless and without an umbrella. She hung her raincoat with the rest, and then turned around and saw me sitting on the far side of the old parlor. She didn't smile, or only a little. She didn't hurry. She crossed toward me with her athlete's walk, a little flat-footed in her sensible shoes. She turned her head in the way women have that tells you they don't want to be kissed on the lips, just good pals. So I put my cheek to hers and felt the cold raindrops caught in her hair.

"You don't fool me, kid," I whispered. "You're hot as a two-dollar pistol."

Now she smiled. "Come on," she said. "Let's have lunch first."

We went from the parlor into the dining room. As we crossed to an empty table, people at four other tables said hello to her. "You're a celebrity," I said once we were settled.

"No, just a lobbyist," she said. She was also, as head of the Washington office of the American Civil Liberties Union, a testifier before Congress, an office manager, a fund-raiser, a TV expert guest, a debater, a speaker, a publicist, and even now and then the lawyer that she had started out being.

"When do you have to start lobbying again?"

"I told Judy I wouldn't be back till three."

"Good thinking." It was five past twelve.

"I'm not really too hungry," Hope said. "Maybe just a cup of soup and a salad. One of the small ones."

"The little garden salad, right? Eat and run?"

"Right."

Not much more than twenty minutes later I had finished my lunch and left the dining room. Hope stalled a few minutes over her coffee and then took the back stairs up to my room. This time she didn't offer me her cheek.

"Two-dollar pistol, huh?" she said, exploring. "Yeah, I see what you mean."

Later, as it was coming up on three o'clock, Hope said, "How long can you stay in Washington?"

"Long as you want. What I'm doing, there's no hurry on it."

"A couple of my board members will be in town tomorrow, so I'll have to babysit with them all day. But Thursday we could see each other."

"Same time, same station?"

"Sure. They do a good garden salad here, don't you think?"

"Yeah, I like it a lot. Actually, I love it. What about Friday, too?"

"That's the thing. I've got to fly to Chicago to fill in for Norm Dorsen at a conference. I just learned this morning."

"I thought Norm stepped down."

"He did, but he's been booked for this for a year and yesterday he broke his damned foot."

"Clumsy son of a bitch."

"A cab ran over it."

"Well, you're supposed to pull your feet out of the way. That's what I've always done."

Hope had been putting her clothes back on and was now talking through hairpins as she reassembled her hair in her usual loose bun. "But you'll be driving through on the way back?" she said.

"Oh, yes," I said, getting up and going over to where she sat in front of the dressing table mirror. "I won't be down in Houston long, all that sun. I'm worried about the ozone layer." I bent over and blew a little puff into her ear.

"You paying attention?" I whispered. She nodded, looking at me in the mirror with my lips to her ear.

"I do, you know," I whispered. "I really, really do."

"I do, too," she said past her hairpins. "I really, really do."

"Get out of here," I said, straightening up.

"I'm gone," Hope said, getting ready to press the last couple of hairpins home. "Practically, anyway. You better get going, too. Justice at three-forty-five, and you don't want to be late. He's off at four-fifteen."

"Justice they close up shop at four-fifteen?"

"He's on flextime."

"You want me to ask, but I won't."

"Good. Then I won't tell you flextime means all the government departments are on staggered shifts. It's so they can make rush hour last longer."

Hope put on her raincoat. From the door, she said, "Thursday. And I still do."

"I do, too," I said to her, and then she was gone. "Really, really," I said to the closed door. It was a law, as far as I could tell, that nobody ever gets married to the right person.

I barely made it to the Justice Department for my appointment. Washington cabs disappear when it rains, even in the middle of the afternoon. By the time one finally stopped, I knew I had made a mistake. I should have taken my own car out of the garage on Rhode

Island Avenue and paid tribute to another parking mafioso. At least I would have been dry.

The cabbie took me to what used to be the side entrance of the Justice Department. The real front entrance is on Pennsylvania Avenue, though. Nixon padlocked it for security reasons during the days of the Vietnam War draft riots. It stayed locked till Carter reopened it to the public. Then paranoia came back to the White House with Reagan, and it was padlocked again. Probably very sensible. If I had been Ed Meese, I'd figure people were out to get me, too.

The man Hope had fixed me up with was on the third floor, down a lot of long corridors and in an office that turned out to be a cubicle. His name was on his desk, inscribed onto one of those prism-shaped pieces of wood that military men and other bureaucrats have on their desks until they get enough rank to have a sign on the office door. The nameplate on the desk said "Pfc. Mark Wilson, HQ & HQ Co., 1st RB&L Bn."

"Vietnam?" I asked, since the bald-headed man who got up behind the desk was about the right age.

"Yeah, I was a Saigon warrior." We shook, and his hand was solid. He was fat, but fat like a two-hundred-pound running guard turns fat. His tie was loose, and he wore a vest, flopping open.

"What's first RB and L."

"The first Radio Broadcasting and Leaflet Battalion. Our unit mission was to bullshit the enemy to death."

"Probably worked as good as what we did in Laos."

"Laos, huh? We'll talk about that. Sit down, sit down."

I sat, which put me right in front of a silver-framed photo that showed a pretty, blond mother and three handsome, perfect blond kids. Two boys and a girl. "Good-looking family you've got," I said.

"Actually my two daughters look a little bit like Arctic seal pups. They take after my ex-wife in that respect, although not otherwise, thank God."

"So who's this?"

"Shit, I don't know. They were in the frame when I bought it at Woodward and Lothrop's."

"How do your kids like it?"

Wilson looked at me for a moment and then smiled. "That's the first intelligent reaction anyone's ever had to that picture," he said. "Actually my kids don't mind it. They know perfectly well that Daddy's crazy, and they know I've got this in my drawer." He handed me another photograph, this one showing two pretty little girls who didn't look anything at all like Arctic seal pups.

"They're cuter than the ones you've got out," I said.

"That's why I don't have 'em out. Same reason I won't have a Harvard sticker on the rear window of my car when they go off to Harvard."

"Makes sense."

"Not to my superiors, it doesn't. It pisses them off something awful. That and the Pfc sign there."

"What's wrong with the sign?"

"They were all officers. They think I'm making fun of officers."

"You are, aren't you?"

"Sure I am. But what pisses them off even more than that is there's not a goddamned thing they can do about it. Like we used to say in Saigon, what are they going to do to me? Send me to Vietnam? They've already got me in the smallest, shittiest office in the building, and I don't seem to care. They can't fire me because I'm civil service, a headless nail. Once I'm pounded in, it's impossible to get me out. And besides, the Young Republican pricks that run this joint know that if there's

23

anybody I hate worse than them, it's the thieves they want me to bite in the ass."

"S and L thieves, Hope said."

"S and L thieves, corporate raiders, inside traders, investment bankers, any kind of white trash that hides loot from Uncle."

"Aren't all those guys Young Republicans, too?"

"Oh, yeah, but tough noogies, fella. That's the way the Republicans do it. They throw one of their pals out of the sleigh to the wolves now and then. The idea is to keep the voters from noticing that the whole goddamned government has been run by and for white-collar criminals for more than a decade. Here, let me show you something. I carry this around to make myself popular with my bosses."

Wilson pulled a worn filing card out of a vest pocket and handed it to me. Typed on it was:

> The English banker wants to know, first, whether your project is sound; second, are you honest; third, are you competent; fourth, is the interest rate satisfactory. Settle these points, and you get your money in twenty-four hours. The American banker asks, first, will the security cover the loan twice over; second, what is the biggest interest rate we can get; third, how are we going to make this devil reorganize his business so we can take it away from him.
>
> —Albert Jay Nock, 1932.

"The only thing changed," Wilson said, "is that since 1932 the English bankers have gotten just as bad as ours. And neither of them cares anymore if the security covers the loan, as long as it's a big loan."

"Who's Albert Jay Nock?"

"He wrote a book called *The Memoirs of a Superflu-*

ous Man. Already you've got to like the guy, don't you? Title like that?"

Already I did. I made a mental note of the title, to see if I could run it down later. Even if it wasn't in print, certainly the Widener would have it.

"Well, look," Wilson said, "it's four o'clock already. I get off at four-fifteen, theoretically. Actually, nobody gives a shit. But any time I schedule a meeting with somebody I don't know, I make it for quarter of four. That way we can stalk around and sniff at each other's tail for a while. If the guy smells kind of off to me, I tell him I've got to meet my carpool. But the fact is I take the Metro, so why don't we hike over to the Old Post Office Building. You know what they've done to it now? No? Well, they fixed it up like a sort of yuppie mall inside, but at least we can get a beer or two while we talk about your problems."

The place turned out to be that saddest of all things, a mall without people. You felt lonely in the open spaces. But the shops and restaurants were all open, hopeful. Over a couple bottles of Sam Adams, I gave Wilson an idea of what I was after, without naming names. I was pretty sure that there wouldn't be any legal way to get the old men's money back from the wreckage of Dr. Somerville's multibillion-dollar empire, and I didn't want Wilson to connect me later with any illegal way I might come up with. So I kept my questions general.

"Hiding assets," the attorney said when I was done. "Interesting field, more interesting every day. Electronic global village stuff. Very hard to detect, even harder to recover. In the real world, there's only one way to go after that kind of money. You ever hunt?"

"A little, as a kid. No more."

"Yeah, you grow out of it if you're worth a shit. My

old man never did. He'd take me out after bear where we lived, out in Arizona. I loved it, back then. Way you hunt a bear, you load up your vehicles with dogs. Two dogs, a bear will tear them up. Three or four might bay him, but they won't tree him. You get nine dogs on that son of a bitch, though, and you'll tree him all right. So you take spare dogs along with you in the jeeps to relieve the tired ones. You let loose a new batch every now and then, and just follow along till they tree him."

"How can you follow in a jeep if the bear is running all over the mountains?" I asked.

"You've got transmitters on the dogs' collars."

"Sounds kind of unfair."

"Well, that's why there's more people than bears. It's also why I wouldn't go out hunting with my dad anymore, after I got to be fourteen or so. Of course if I had anything against bears, it would be different. I wouldn't mind setting the dogs on most of the customers I get at the office. These people are real slime."

"Personally or in the abstract?"

"Personally, most of them. Although some of them can be awful goddamned charming, awful smooth. But what they all leave after them is ruined companies, ruined industries, now a ruined economy. You know what those former goddamned Masters of the Universe used to call it when they loaded some corporation down with debt and fired thousands of people to pay off the debt? Body rain. They were using the jobs of human beings to buy the companies with.

"Fuck 'em, that's all. Bastards like that, I'm going to use every goddamned dog I can get. Which brings me back to the point. You're asking two questions here. One is finding the money that these pricks have rat-holed away. Like I said, that's tough, very tough. The other question is after you find the money, how do you get them to disgorge it? That's what the law calls it, cute word. Disgorgement is also tough.

"But what I can do, and you as a private citizen can't, is I can let loose every possible dog on one of these pricks. FBI dogs, IRS dogs, judge dogs with court orders. If I can, I'll get the state or local prosecutors and cops after the guy. I'll get the EPA, the transit police, the zoning commission, I don't give a shit who, I'll get them after him. I'll have him fighting ten, fifteen dogs at once if I can. And I'll tree him, count on it. Then, knowing the realities of how the court system operates, I'll holler up to the son of a bitch and cut a deal. 'Hey, bear,' I'll say. 'Tell me where you got your honey stashed, maybe I'll let you down from that tree and then call the dogs off. Right after I let them have a bite or two of your ass for the sake of office morale. Just to make my dogs feel like all that running was worth it.' Which is the Boesky and Milken cases in a nutshell."

I said, "So you're telling me the bear always wins unless you've got a lot of dogs."

"That's what I'm telling you."

I wondered what he'd tell me if he knew my bear was dead.

Wilson was a drinker, and I drank right along with him—both because he was good company and because I had nothing else to do except think about Hope at home with her husband and kids. By the time he was ready to head for the Metro we had each put away five beers. It wasn't even seven o'clock yet, as I was surprised to learn when I looked at my throwaway Casio. "Suppose there'd be any bookstores still open?" I asked.

"Probably the big chains. Crown Books, like that. What are you looking for?"

"The one you were talking about. The superfluous man one."

"Used books, I guess. What part of town you staying?"

"The Tabard."

"Yeah, that's right, you said. Try Second Story Books on P. Around Twentieth, Twenty-first. Just west of the circle, anyway."

I left Wilson at the Federal Triangle Metro station, a bulky figure in a flimsy, dingy raincoat that had probably lost its waterproofing long ago. He had an umbrella, but it didn't look like much, either. The fabric had pulled loose from one of the spokes, and the next good gust would probably finish the job. He didn't look like much to send up against the Masters of the Universe—but he could command the dogs, and the Boeskys and the Milkens couldn't.

Wilson was probably going home to knock back another half-dozen beers before, during, and after supper, the way I used to myself. But in those days I was both a married man and a serious drinker. Now I was unmarried and had more of a grip on the drinking. Five beers in less than two hours would have been a warm-up once. No more. Now I had reached my dose. In fact I was a little over it, which was why I hadn't taken the Metro myself. The cold and the rain would do me good. I fastened the various tabs and buttons on my oiled-canvas Driza-bone coat and set out through the windy, mostly deserted streets toward Dupont Circle.

By the time I had covered the twenty blocks or so, my socks were squishy and the bottoms of my pants legs were heavy, wet, and shapeless. But the calf-length coat had kept the rest of my clothes dry. The clerk hadn't heard of the book anymore than I had a few hours before, and so I poked around on my own. After a while I found a book by Albert Jay Nock, all right, but not the right one. It was called *Our Enemy, the State*, which showed promise as a title. Not twenty-eight dollars' worth of promise, though, even if it was a first edition. The only point to a real book is to wrestle around in the margins with the author, and I wouldn't feel comfortable scribbling on a twenty-eight-dollar first edition.

I had better luck at Kramerbooks, a store I came across on my way back to the Tabard. *Memoirs of a Superfluous Man* was still in print, it turned out, and the clerk took me to a paperback copy. The opening sentence was, "It has several times been suggested to me, always to my great annoyance, that I should write an autobiography." After reading that, I had to buy the book. It was the only way to see how he had managed to get the better of his annoyance.

Back in the hotel room, I hung up my coat to drip. I was still mostly dry, but my feet were cold and clammy enough so that I put them to bed. I turned on the reading light and pulled up the covers and opened my new book and then the literary urge left me. Hope's smell was still in the bed. Five bottles of Sam Adams were still metabolizing in my system. I began to feel sorry for myself, and it didn't help to remember that when I had had a wife and a baby of my own to go home to, during my bush pilot days in Alaska, I was generally out drinking with the boys instead.

It was much too early to go to sleep, but I did it anyway. It was better than thinking. Next morning, awake at five o'clock, I turned on the light and opened my new book. It was still dark out, from the overcast that was covering the East Coast, when I went down for breakfast at seven-thirty.

I had a nine-thirty appointment that Mark Wilson had set up for me, with a man at the Internal Revenue Service who specialized in money laundering, concealment of assets, and offshore banking. He led me to a couple of committee staffers on Capitol Hill, and they pointed me to a woman who wrote on business for the *Washington Post*. I told all of them I was doing research on government regulation of cash transactions for an author in Boston. I didn't mention Dr. Denton Somerville, or Sunbanc Savings and Loan, or even Houston. Just as with Wilson, I didn't want them connecting my name with any news that might come out of Texas later. Whatever I wound up doing down there, it wasn't likely to be under court order. I didn't have those dogs on my side.

Hope came for lunch Thursday, and again I enjoyed the ripple effect as she passed through the parlor and into the dining room with me, people who knew her saying hello and people who wished they did just following her with their eyes. Hope was good-looking, if I tried to be objective about it, but not a world-class beauty. What drew people's eyes, I imagined, was her air of health, emotional as well as physical. At just the sight of her, you figured she was comfortable with her personality and physique, and confident of both. A woman like her would never have any trouble going to sleep at night, you'd think, and in fact she didn't.

After lunch we took our time over a pot of coffee for her and a pot of tea for me, instead of rushing upstairs in a starved hurry the way we had on Tuesday. Now we were calmed-down, civilized people, with time to smell the roses.

"What have you been up to, Bethany?" Hope asked as she poured.

"Well, your friend Wilson sent me to some people, and they sent me to some others, so now I'm an expert in concealment of assets."

"What do you know about it?"

"I know it's pretty easy to do."

"Which means the assets are pretty tough to find."

"Very tough."

"So what are you going to do?"

"I'll drive south till I get to some sun. Houston was eighty-two today, according to the weatherman. Then see if I can find any of Dr. Denton's money still lying around."

"What if you do?"

"Got no plans. I don't know enough yet to have any."

"Is there a Mrs. Dr. Denton?"

"Somewhere, yeah. She was holding on to his arm in some of the pictures in the papers. But no mention of her since he had his heart attack and died. After what I've read about him, I'm surprised he had a heart."

"If he put the money in his wife's name, your old men up in Cambridge will never see it."

"No, probably not."

"I don't like the sound of that probably, Bethany. Do you have something in mind?"

"Not a thing."

"Honestly?"

"Honestly."

"Well, I do. Go on upstairs and I'll be up in a few minutes."

3

THE NEXT DAY I SAT AROUND my room reading till midmorning. It didn't make much difference when I left. The reports were that it would still be cold and raining whatever time I took off, as well as through the weekend. Hope was out when I called her office. I left the message that a Tom Bethany had called, and would try again Monday.

I got as far as Bristol, on the Virginia-Tennessee line, before the knots in my neck and shoulders drove me off Interstate 81 and to shelter. It had taken me something like ten hours to cover the distance, which was only about 360 miles. All the way I was running with my lights on, leaning forward and squinting to see through the rain, blinded regularly by the wash of passing trucks. Except for around Charlottesville, there didn't seem to be a decent radio station in the entire Commonwealth of Virginia. I tried my tapes for a while, but even good music turned out to be sensory overload. To handle the rain, the gusty crosswinds, the swishing of the wipers, and the bright blurs of headlights on the eighteen-wheelers took all the concentration I had.

The trip as far as Washington had been on my nickel, but now I was spending the money of the twelve old men in Cambridge. So I fell naturally back into the cheap ways that I had learned while a G.I. Bill student at the University of Iowa and while training to make the Olympic wrestling team the year after graduation. I made the team, but Carter boycotted the Moscow summer games to make Brezhnev really sorry he ever invaded Afghanistan. It probably didn't make Brezhnev sorry at all, though, since it meant his jocks wound up winning most of the gold medals. Next time we won any was on Reagan's watch, timed just right to help him beat Mondale.

During most of my wrestling years, I had had no choice but to live on practically nothing. One of the things I learned was how to travel on the very minimum. Most people blow it before they even start the trip, by buying an expensive car. My car cost me $400 when I bought it from a divinity student five years ago, and it was five years old then. Even after what I pay the boys at MacKinnon Motors to keep the thing in perfect running order, my per-mile cost is a fraction of the hit you take if you drive a new car. The second big lesson is that since no motel room is really comfortable, the only important difference between them is money. So I hunted out a $19.95 cheapo in Bristol and offered the clerk $15 in cash. He took it, since most of the rooms were empty. Possibly, too, since cash leaves no tracks.

The room smelled musty, which was unimportant. You stop noticing smells after a few minutes, presumably because the brain is programmed to set them aside once evaluated, making room for new smells that could

lead to fight or flight, or food or fornication. Whatever
the reason, I knew that in five minutes the room
wouldn't smell musty to me anymore. There was a color
TV and a phone, both working. There was hot water,
and a roof that didn't leak. Thin blankets and an uncomfortable mattress were on the bed. In all these respects,
my $15 room was identical to a $60 Holiday Inn room
with a new Beautyrest. As I would have done in the
Holiday Inn, too, I opened up the orange nylon equipment bag that carried my motel kit. It held a couple of
extra blankets, a couple of extra pillows, and a 200-watt
bulb. With this supplemental gear, I could prop myself
up, read, and stay warm all at the same time. Which I
did, once I had spent ten minutes letting a hot shower
deal with the kinks in my neck and shoulders.

It was still raining when I left the next day, but by
the time I picked up Interstate 40 at Knoxville the sun
was coming through now and then. By Nashville the sky
was blue and the sun was bright. My whole outlook
began to change from pessimism to optimism. Down in
Houston, Dr. Somerville's heirs were no doubt ashamed
of what he had done and would hand me a satchel full
of money to take back to the Dummy Dozen. What's
more, as soon as I delivered the money I would begin
at last to work my way through the Harvard Classics, all
fifty volumes. I would eat more fruit and fiber. I'd learn
to iron my own shirts. I'd learn something about classi-
cal music. As if God heard me, a Wal-Mart came into
view, easy-off. I could get started on my program right
now.

For $3.99 each, I bought tapes called *The Best of Bach*,
The Best of Beethoven, and *The Best of Mozart*. All three
men had good reputations, but I bought *Peggy Lee: The
Early Years* as a backup, just in case. Easy-on, I was
soon rolling west along Interstate 40 again, listening to

"Air on the G-String," from Suite No. 3 in D. It seemed okay, although it was a couple loads shy of being Peggy Lee. I stopped for the night somewhere east of Memphis, early enough to get in a four-mile run before nightfall. After my run I found a supermarket and bought a jar of grapefruit juice, a bunch of bananas, and a pound or so of peanuts in the shell. That probably took care of fruit and fiber, although I wasn't entirely clear on how much fiber there was in a peanut.

I read my book in bed, underlining as I went along. Mr. Nock had an unusual take on a lot of things. Universal literacy, for instance. "It makes many articulate who should not be so," he wrote. "It puts into a people's hands an instrument which very few can use, but which everyone supposes himself fully able to use; and the mischief thus wrought is very great."

Sure enough, along comes Reagan forty years later, reading from his file cards. Mr. Nock wouldn't have been surprised. "Before you can have an ideal republic you must have ideal republicans," he had written. And, "As against a Jesus, the historic choice of the mass-man goes regularly to some Barabbas." And, "I have often thought it might be amusing to write a humorous essay on how to recognise the Dark Ages when you are in them."

I could have helped him on that. You're in them when your country is hip-deep in yellow ribbons and the only sensible voices left come from Russell Baker and Doonesbury and "Saturday Night Live." In fact it was Saturday night now, and just about that time, so I set my book aside and jumped into the tube for a while before going off to sleep.

Houston was too much of a drive to make in a day unless you were in a hurry, so on Sunday I aimed for Texarkana and stopped late in the afternoon a little south of there. Monday, moving along easily, I headed down into Texas. The sun was still shining, but the slight chill of the previous day was gone. I had been in Texas before, but never the part with trees. The leaves were just showing yellow-green. Maybe everything would dry up and turn brown in the summer, but right now it was pleasant country once you looked past the usual roadside ugliness. The principal local industry was junk, it looked like. The dealers called their businesses flea markets. Explosions of trash for sale ran along Route 59 as if the area had been carpet-bombed with old washing machines, stoves, furniture, hubcaps, and rusty power mowers.

Eventually the countryside disappeared entirely as I approached Houston. I passed a few motels that looked cheap, but I knew they wouldn't be. The thrifty traveler stays away from places that say COUPLES on the sign. You've got to figure on condom machines in the lobby, noisy neighbors, and, worst of all, hourly rates. I left the freeway once I got in the general area of a few skyscrapers that stuck out of the urban sprawl. Since the elevated highway had been running for ten miles or so through neighborhoods of mostly two- or three-story buildings, I figured the high-rises must signify some sort of downtown.

They didn't signify motels, though. I wandered around more or less at random for an hour, sometimes trying to find myself on my map of Houston but not worrying too much when I couldn't. The city was kind of interesting. Three million people had spread themselves out over a flat pancake of land maybe twenty miles wide. The invisible hand of the real estate market had sprinkled bowling alleys, hospitals, pawnshops, million-dollar homes, car washes, schools, skyscrapers, parking lots, churches, over the whole pancake pretty much at random. I drove through a couple of blocks of low, fancy houses shaded by live oaks, then immediately into a commercial strip with two cellular phone stores, a gym, an animal hospital, a couple of palm readers, a bookstore, and a muffler shop. Then more expensive homes, with here and there a taxidermist's or a maternity shop among them, and so on. The city was laid out like a pizza with everything.

This was because Houston, unlike most cities, never had any zoning laws. Most cities are planned, like Boston. In Boston you can't just go out and build whatever you want to, anyplace you happen to feel like building it. In Boston you have to pay off first. That's the plan.

After an hour or so of wandering, the thought struck me that the invisible hand of the market might not keep businesses out of residential neighborhoods, but it was likely to keep motels near highways. So I found the feeder road that bordered the Southwest Freeway and explored it. Before long I found a motel with weekly rates that wouldn't hurt my twelve old men too much. I paid in cash for a week, registering as Tom Henderson, the name on my *Boston Globe* press card. I didn't know anybody in Houston, so maybe they wouldn't know anybody in Boston. As long as I stayed away from real newspapermen, I should be all right.

Next morning I set out for Houston's old downtown area, where my map showed that most of the government buildings were. I left the freeway for Louisiana Street, which took me through a mile or so of low sprawl before the skyscrapers started. The weather was pleasant, about right for a light jacket, but practically nobody was on the sidewalks. People probably lost the walking habit, being huddled next to the air conditioner ten months out of the year.

The skyscrapers gave way to what used to make up the downtown area in cities the size Houston used to be: ten- or twelve-story buildings in a wide band running along the water. I parked in an all-day lot for $3.75, which was about what an hour would have cost me in Washington. A few hundred yards away was what passed for waterfront in Houston, Buffalo Bayou. The river didn't seem to have any flow at all. Its mud shoreline was gradually absorbing tons of litter. Most of it was plastic, which should fossilize well.

The old business area was going the way of most old business areas. The gutters and alleys smelled of stale piss. Some of the stores were boarded up. The others were occupied by bail bondsmen, check-cashing services, porn shops, merchants of cheap jewelry and electronics, sandwich shops, and army-navy stores. A few of the city's more successful horse thieves still maintained a presence in the area, though. Back by the bayou was a plain, solid prewar building with a sign on top that read "SOUTHERN PACIFIC." And the *Houston Chronicle* was just down the street from the Golden Star Cinema and its triple-X features. Chiseled into marble outside the *Chronicle's* main entrance were the words of somebody called Jesse H. Jones: "The publication of a newspaper is a distinct public trust and not one to be treated lightly or abused for selfish purposes or to gratify selfish whims. A great daily newspaper can remain a power for good only so long as it is uninfluenced by unworthy motives and unbought by the desire for gain." Jones had to have been The Founder, since nobody else could have got prose that bad onto a wall. And nobody but a newspaper publisher would have been dumb enough to believe it.

The Bob Casey Federal Building was a few blocks farther on. It was a large cube of pockmarked concrete ten stories high, studded with tiny square windows. Each window had a faded maroon border. Without those maroon windows your eyes probably wouldn't register the Bob Casey Federal Building at all—just slide on past, as if it were an A&P distribution center or an airplane hangar. With the maroon, though, you took a closer look and wondered what old Bob had done to get a building that ugly named after him.

A guard told me the way to the clerk's office, and I boarded one of the Bob Casey elevators. "What you been up to?" a man with a string tie said to another man with a string tie as we all rode up.

"Waiting for you to pay me some money," the second man answered. "I figure you must owe me for something."

I got off before they could work it all out, and found the clerk's office. I didn't even need my press card. All I had to do was pick up a wall phone and ask a woman for Denton Somerville's file number. Behind the counter was a maze made by those chest-high dividers that set off the space assigned to one worker-organism from the exactly similar space assigned to the next worker-organism. The file room was beyond this honeycomb. The files were off to the left behind a steel mesh wall. Reading tables were to the right. Once I had signed as Tom Henderson and put down the motel's phone number, a man behind the grille handed me out three folders, each as thick as the Boston yellow pages. I picked out a table, opened my briefcase, took out a spiral notebook, put on my reading glasses, and started plowing through *United States of America v Denton Somerville.*

If I had been interested in the cases themselves, I would have been at it till the end of the week. And I *was* interested in the cases to some extent, but I was more interested in the names and addresses of the various people associated with them. So I was able to get through all three folders before closing time, although not much before. When I handed back the folders, the man behind the grille told me where I could find Miranda Weeks, Esq. To judge from the files, she was the assistant U.S. attorney who seemed to have led the pack that treed Dr. Denton.

The office with her name on the door was up on the next floor. Inside the door was a secretary tidying up her desk, almost ready to clear out. She took my card in to her boss. The boss herself came out. In her stocking feet, which is the way she was, she stood maybe an inch taller than my five eleven. Like so many tall women and white basketball players, she didn't carry the height particularly well. She was somewhere around forty, with a plain face wearing an expression that didn't seem friendly or unfriendly. Just uninterested.

"I'm afraid I can't talk to the press right now," she said. "I have at least an hour's work left to do tonight."

"Whatever time suits you," I said. "I wanted to talk about the Somerville case."

"The nefarious Dr. Denton," she said. Now she looked interested. "I wish I could, but I'm up to here. I didn't even have time for lunch today."

"Neither did I. Why don't I go out and do some errands, and meet you in the lobby at six-thirty? The *Globe* can buy us dinner."

She thought about the different elements of that proposition for a moment, and said, "I could have dinner with you, but I couldn't let the press pay for mine. I think it's better if I pay for my own."

"Fine," I said. Particularly since my old men would have been buying, not the *Globe*.

I killed the hour by reading the newspapers, back at the parking lot. There was a slight chill in the air now that the sun was going down, but nothing like what I had left in Cambridge. Inside the car it was comfortable. The *Houston Post* was in the middle of a no-holds-barred series on "some of the actions and philosophies that go into being Texan." The local hospitality was the thing that was most attractive to new Texans, according to the headline on page one. "I truly believe this state gets its heart from the people," one new Texan said. She was the Houston chief of police, an import from Philadelphia. "So if it's true that everything is bigger in Texas, the hearts of Texans are no exception." A restaurateur from Colombia had tried California for a while, but preferred Texas. "They show more their true colors here than in California," he said. "In California they're not black or white, they're pink, you know?" Actually I didn't know. Maybe it was something to do with the ozone layer. I read on.

A Scottish ballet dancer, the *Post* had discovered, "started feeling like a real Texan 'when I finally mastered y'all,' he announced in a lilting brogue." There was bad news for the dancer on page A-14, though. The *Houston Post* InfoPoll had learned that "To be a true Texan you have to be born in Texas, according to almost 70 percent of the 608 people responding."

And so it went, for column after column, and still the *Post*'s investigative reporters hadn't gotten to the bottom of their subject. At the end, the editors promised, "Tomorrow: Texas sports heroes." I made a note of that, so I could buy the *Chronicle* instead.

I figured my dinner date would be on the dot, and so I was in the lobby of the Bob Casey Federal Building at six twenty-five. In exactly five minutes Miranda Weeks stepped out of the elevator. She wore low-heeled shoes, but they still added another inch to her height. She carried an old-fashioned pigskin briefcase, the kind that bulges.

"I haven't seen a briefcase like that in years," I said, to make talk.

"It belonged to my father, and I didn't see any reason to throw it away when he died," she said. "They hold much more than the new ones."

"Your father a lawyer, too?" I said, still making talk.

"He was disbarred," she said. "Do you like Cajun?"

I said nothing for a beat or two, and then I said, "Cajun . . . Yeah, Cajun's fine."

"There's a good place a few blocks away," Miranda Weeks said. "Real reasonable and big servings. Cafeteria style. All the iced tea or coffee you want. They set urns out so you can help yourself."

The place turned out to be everything she said it was, and the food was good, too. When Miranda Weeks ate, she ate. She didn't say much until she had finished every bit of everything, right down to the last grain of her dirty rice. She let me catch up, and then it was time to talk. "What's your interest in Dr. Somerville?" she asked. "After all, he's dead."

"That's part of the story, actually. Guy cheats the hangman."

"He cheated me, all right. I practically lived with Dr. Somerville for two years, but I can't imagine anybody else being interested at this late date."

"I'm doing it for our Sunday magazine, so it doesn't really have to be news. The thing is, it's got the professional angle. We've got even more doctors in Boston than you've got in Houston. Somerville's somebody they can identify with."

This didn't even sound convincing to me. Time to move on fast, before the ice broke under me. "What sort of a man was he?" I asked.

"I never met him."

"Thought you said—"

"I lived with him by directing the investigation into his violations of the law. Laws. If he had lived, he would have been tried on nineteen different felony counts under six different statutes, carrying a total possible sentence of 316 years. And those were just the felonies I indicted him for. I had others in reserve, but I didn't want to seem to be indulging in overkill."

This didn't seem to be a joke, and so I didn't risk a smile. "Wouldn't you have to meet him to indict him?" I asked.

"Not necessarily. He wouldn't have to appear before the grand jury if he didn't want to, and he didn't. My staff deposed him numerous times, of course, but I was never present. I try to remain uninvolved with defendants so that emotions won't interfere with my conduct of the case."

"From what you knew about him, what kind of a guy was he?"

"Not for attribution?"

"Absolutely. In fact, I'll make a deal with you. Whatever I wind up quoting you on, I'll let you look at before it goes in the paper."

"Isn't that an unusual procedure?"

"Not for me. I'd rather go with exactly what the person meant to say, not what they may have said by mistake and then have second thoughts about it."

"Not for attribution, then, Denton Somerville was contemptible."

"Can you give me a for instance?"

"I could give them to you all day, but let me just tell you about one. In one of our depositions, a close friend and associate of Dr. Somerville's said he asked him one day how he could cheat people who trusted him, and you know what the man answered?"

I did, because it's an old line. But I shook my head.

"He said that's the only kind of people you *could* cheat."

"I guess that's true, when you think about it," I said. "What kind of a close friend would tell prosecutors a story like that, though?"

"A close friend who wanted to stay out of jail. We gave immunity to half the white-collar thieves in Houston to get them to testify against Somerville, and now we can't touch any of them."

"Did you give immunity to Harmon H. Harmon?"

"Harmon? Oh, Dr. Somerville's driver. I remember the odd name, and the *H* stands for Harmon, too. I never think it's a very good idea to give children names like that."

I was about to tell her that one of my sisters was christened Beth Bethany and still thinks it's real cute. But I remembered in time that I was Thomas G. Henderson right at the moment.

"Anyway, the answer to your question is no," Weeks went on. "We offered him immunity but he wouldn't accept it. He said he hadn't done anything wrong and didn't need it. He wasn't responsive to our questions, though."

"I read his deposition," I said. "He developed instant Alzheimer's, sounded like. I wondered why."

"Very intelligent on his part. I suspect Mr. Harmon isn't quite as simple as he probably seemed to you from that deposition. He hadn't retained counsel as far as I know, but he seemed to know exactly how to handle prosecutorial questioning."

"What I wondered was why would he bother to develop amnesia?" I said. "After all, here's a guy that lost his shirt buying Dr. Dentons with payroll deductions."

"Dr. Denton's what?"

"Those uninsured bonds he got the suckers to swap their insured accounts for. Some of the newspapers called them Dr. Dentons because basically they weren't worth more than a pair of Dr. Dentons."

"Oh, Dr. Dentons like the children's underwear. I see."

"So what I'm wondering is why Harmon would protect his boss when his boss was ripping him off every Friday."

"Perhaps because Harmon didn't blame his boss. Harmon would assume his employer couldn't know that the bonds would turn out to be worthless."

"All the papers said Somerville knew. In fact the stories said he set up the umbrella corporation for that exact reason. So he could loot the S and L and make those bonds worthless."

"But the papers said those things *after* we deposed Mr. Harmon," Miranda Weeks said. "At the time of the deposition, he probably thought his boss was operating in good faith."

"I guess that's possible," I said. "Till it came out in the papers later, he might not have known that the whole point of those bonds was so Somerville could transfer the S and L's money into his own pockets. Which brings up another thing. When hundreds of millions of bucks disappear like that, where do they go?"

"I really don't know. When Dr. Somerville died, my task force very frankly moved on to other S and L crooks. We haven't devoted any resources to tracking down the missing money, but I imagine his wife, Billene Somerville, wound up with a lot of it. The typical pattern with these people is to set up trusts in the names of the wives and the children. That way you keep control of the money, but creditors can't get at it."

"Where's the wife?"

"I don't really know."

"What's she like?"

"I never paid much attention. The best place to find out about people in Billene's world would be from Jim Bill Pennington. He's some kind of poor cousin to both the Cullens and the Hobbys, so he went to all the cotillions around the same time Billene would have. He's a history professor at Rice University now."

"You think he'd talk to me?"

"That's why I mentioned him, Mr. Henderson. Talking is what Jim Bill *does*."

"Call me Tom," I said. "I feel more comfortable with that."

Which was certainly the truth. I hadn't got used to Henderson yet. We talked for another ten minutes about the man who got away, but what she knew was in general what I knew, too, from the courthouse and newspaper files on Somerville. What I liked best so far was the chauffeur. First time out I hadn't paid much attention to the Harmon H. Harmon testimony, which for forgetfulness was in a class with Reagan's deposition on Iran-Contra. But he might have his memory back by now.

Once we were outside the restaurant I offered to walk Miranda Weeks back to her car. "That won't be necessary," she said, hefting her briefcase. "I carry a gun."

I thought about her setting a briefcase down, unlocking it, and finding a gun inside it while an attacker waited. But maybe it didn't matter. She didn't look like the kind of woman who would accost easy. I went to my own car and headed back to the motel. I found a number for a J. W. Pennington in the directory and gave it a try.

"Want to grab supper someplace?" he said when I had

identified myself. "Oh, you have? With old Miranda, huh? She's fun on a date, isn't she? I'm just shitting with you, you understand? Miranda's good people. Now listen, how about two-thirty tomorrow afternoon? You want to take a little ride with me? Good, now here's where you come to . . ."

4

GODDAMN IF YOU HAVEN'T
got a worse car than I do," Professor Pennington said
when he saw my Datsun in the parking lot outside his
office the next day. "Know what I like best about that
pitiful, spavined little son of a bitch you got there? You
haven't got a yellow ribbon on it. Goddamn, I just *love*
a car without a yellow ribbon. Come on, let's go. We'll
show those pricks in River Oaks what a car's supposed
to look like. Goddamn, you got whale stickers on her,
too. They're gonna flat love this car. Turn left out of the
parking lot, pedal to the metal. Don't worry about a
thing. Car like this, you can do ninety-five and never get
a ticket in this town. Not with Massachusetts plates and
that Greenpeace sticker on the bumper. They're all envi-
ronmentalists, Houston cops."

He had me pull into a Stop-N-Go, and I watched him
disappear inside. Pennington wore the top to long johns
and over it a button-down shirt of blue oxford cloth

laundered soft. The shirt was open at the neck and rolled up at the sleeves, so that his undershirt showed. He was only forty or so, but already a substantial belly pooched out over his low-slung Levi's. He had thin legs and no butt to speak of, so that he looked like a fat person joined at the belt line to a skinny one. His hair was going fast. What there was of it was blond and lank and six weeks overdue for a trim. He didn't look much like a Harvard professor, but I figured he probably didn't look much like a Rice one, either. When he came back he was carrying a big paper bag.

"Got a couple six-packs," he said as he off-loaded them onto the floor in back. "Probably more than we need just to look at River Oaks, but beer keeps. Let me tell you something about River Oaks, so as you'll understand what you're seeing. What it is basically is a housing development, thrown up, you might say, just in time for the Great Depression. Now the crucial thing you got to understand, it was modeled after Shaker Heights. You know Shaker Heights?"

"Outside Cleveland, isn't it?"

"You got it. Which means the cream of Houston society lives in a rip-off of a Cleveland suburb. Probably that explains a lot, but I'll be goddamned if I can figure what."

River Oaks wasn't too far from my motel, it turned out, and we rolled along in light midday traffic till we came up on something to the right that looked like the entrance to a city park. "That's the River Oaks Country Club," Pennington said. "Take a left here and we'll drive through the slave quarters before I show you Somerville's little place."

What he called slave quarters were half-million-dollar houses in the low-rent portions of the subdivision. And in fact they weren't that impressive. I wondered why people that rich would want to live right on top of one another. My bum of a father had more property than that back in Port Henry, New York, although he landscaped it with junked cars instead of azaleas and rhododendrons.

"Take a left here," Pennington said. "This is Inwood Street, lot of royals live here. Some of my Cullen cousins, used to be. Howard Hughes, too. That's our idea of royalty here in Houston, Howard Hughes. Crazy son of a bitch shuffling around his penthouse with Kleenex boxes on his feet for slippers. Okay, right up there's the old Somerville place, part of Houston history. Been standing on that exact same spot since 1985."

"Doesn't look new," I said.

"It shouldn't," Pennington said. "Not after all the dough Denton spent on making it look old. Of course the trees help. In fact the trees are the whole point."

The Somerville mansion was enormous and had an understated suggestion of New England about it. The ancestral Somerville trees were mostly huge live oaks hung with Spanish moss. There were pin oaks and water oaks, too, and loblolly pine. The understory was holly, magnolias, crepe myrtle, dogwood, and redbud. The redbud was in bloom. So were daffodils and azaleas.

"There used to be a Frank Lloyd Wright house here," Pennington said. "Ugly goddamned thing, but I repeat myself. Denton bought the place for the trees and the cellar hole, basically. He figured the house was a teardown, that's what they call it here when you buy a house just for the lot and tear it down to make room for the new one. Only the historical commission, fine arts commission, some damned thing, said it was a landmark and he couldn't touch it. So as far as I know for sure, he didn't. He was in the Bahamas with Billene a couple weeks later when it burned down. The goo-goos fussed about it for a while, but there wasn't a thing they could do."

"Wouldn't the insurance company wonder about it?"

"He bought it for a tear-down. They're not going to insure a tear-down. Now up to this point we've got a typical Houston story, although I got to say the fire was going a little far. But then Denton moved right up into the Saudi Arabian class. He spent three million dollars buying the properties on both sides, and he tore those down, too. Put that swimming pool there in one of the foundation holes, but mostly he just wanted a bigger lot."

"Who lives in his place now?"

"Nobody. Real estate isn't moving too fast right now."

"No sign out front."

"You can't put FOR SALE signs up in River Oaks. It's a deed restriction. Wasn't for that, every third house we drove by would have had a sign on the lawn."

"Were you ever inside the Somerville place?"

"Oh, sure. I'm not on the A list, because I don't have any money. But I'm on the B list because I'm a professor at Rice and my middle name is Cullen. So they let me wear bells on my cap and entertain the quality."

"What's the place like?"

"Way above most of them, I'll tell you. Denton had some nice things. He had one room furnished entirely with custom-made Shaker reproductions from Ian Ingersoll's shop up in Connecticut. Had some good paintings, too. Which is unusual, considering that Houston's idea of art is Frederic Remington or some ugly piece of shit by Picasso that everybody pretends to like because it cost so much money. But Denton collected American portraits, mostly early nineteenth century. Some good stuff by Neagle and Inman, the first time anybody in Houston ever heard of them.

"It was kind of amusing, really. Somerville came down here from up north and beat the game by not playing it. Instead of buying lizard skin boots and Armani suits, he rented a suite in the Hilton out at the Medical Center for J. Press and had them send a tailor down from New Haven to measure him. Pretty soon all the other doctors were going over there to be measured, too. Then a lot of the old guard started to show up for fittings, and you started to see unpadded shoulders all over town. You'd've thought you were at goddamned Andover.

"His house was the same way. He hired Benson Ford to build it to order for him. Ford went up to Rhode Island or someplace to make copies of just the right kinds of moldings, window latches, doorknobs, every fucking thing. Did it right, too, I got to say. Didn't try to make it look original. Just reproduced things exactly, brand-new except for the flooring. Apparently you can't get planks anymore as wide as the ones the colonists used, so Ford had to buy them out of demolished houses or barns. Then at last everything was finished and Denton opened his new house up and said, There she is, folks, eat your heart out. And damned if they didn't."

Pennington laughed, delighted. He took a long pull at his third beer of the outing. I was on my first. "I never knew if the son of a bitch was a phony or not," he said. "For all I know, he was a scholarship boy at Andover and Brown. Maybe his old man drove a garbage truck. But Denton sure carried it off. Lot of Yankees come down here, they develop a drawl inside of six months. Old Denton went the other way. He came down here with the Long Island lockjaw, and the longer he stayed, the worse it got."

"What about his wife?"

"She talked Texas."

"I meant what was she like?"

"Well, how she talked is how she was. Third-generation timber and oil money from East Texas. She went to Kincaid School, then SMU. Pi Phi at SMU. Past president of the Cotillion Club of Houston. That's Billene."

"What kind of name is Billene?"

"Billene is the kind of name you give a girl who has a total asshole named Bill for a father, and he wanted a boy."

"Pretty tough on the kid."

"Oh, she didn't mind it. She has her father's brains."

"From what I read about him, Somerville was a smart son of a bitch."

"Yeah, but that didn't mean he wanted a smart wife. He struck me as a man that needed to be adored twenty-four hours a day. Instant obedience. Total submersion of the wife's ego in his. She'd look at him with this goddamned Nancy Reagan gaze, and old Denton, he'd just eat it up where a normal man would have puked after a week or two of it.

"Doesn't mean he wasn't sharp, though, old Denton. He damned sure was. But she was just as thick as whaleshit. Now and then if she said something unusually moronic, he'd kind of correct her politely, and she'd back right off. But mostly he'd just listen to her babble away and smile like she was just the cutest, brightest little thing he had ever heard of. In a way it was kind of touching, but in a way it was kind of sick, too. I mean, with everybody else he was a cold, vicious son of a bitch."

"Was she a son of a bitch, too?"

"Not really, not particularly mean. She was just what her daddy raised her to be, a spoiled, manipulative, dependent little southern belle. That's the way we raise 'em, because that's the way we like 'em. In the best of 'em the training doesn't take, of course, but an empty skull like Billene's, you can dump anything you want into it."

I thought of the pictures of the Somervilles I had seen, grainy newspaper pictures that showed up even worse on the microfilm projectors than they had on the page. Billene was small and must have made a cute cheer-leader. The cute giving way to pretty in her twenties, probably, and to attractive now that she was moving on toward forty. Before long people would be calling her "still attractive." Human life, from an ex-cheerleader's point of view anyway, would be over.

"Was she a cheerleader?" I asked.

"Better damn well believe it. Cheerleading is what gals like Billene are bred for. Egging on adolescent males to fight, with her as the prize."

"Liked the boys, did she?"

"Oh, she liked them, all right. But you know some-thing? It wouldn't surprise me a bit if she was a virgin when she married Denton. Old southern tradition, not going all the way. I knew a couple of football players used to go out with her at SMU, and they told me she was saving it for her husband. By 'it' I mean her techni-cal virginity. Didn't mean she wouldn't go down on any-thing that wore a jockstrap. Which of course both of my buddies did. What they told me, old Billene could suck-start a Harley."

The newspaper pictures showed that Dr. Denton had been fairly tall, but definitely a little pudgy. "Somerville doesn't look much like he ever wore a jockstrap," I said.

"No, I don't believe he ever did. But an M.D. is pretty near as good with the girls. Tell you something, too. You take some nerd out of Tufts Medical School and set a gal loose on him that practiced up on the whole SMU backfield and you know what you got? What you got, son, is instant love."

"A couple of scorpions that found each other, huh?"

"Well, Billene didn't really start out being a scorpion. She started out being a hunk of wax. She just took her shape from whatever man was pressing down on her. You might say."

I tried to imagine the two of them, childless and all alone with each other in the enormous house. Servants, presumably, but still. "They do much entertaining?" I asked.

"Not as much as you'd think. Most guys in that line of work, they're basically salesmen. Out with the boys all the time. But Denton, he'd stay home nights. Played a lot of gin rummy, the two of them, what I understand. Watch movies. Had their own little movie theater in there, watched whatever they wanted on the big screen. That's the only thing I really envied the son of a bitch for. You take a flick like *Texas Chainsaw Massacre*, it frankly ain't worth shit on the VCR. In fact you got to see it in the drive-in, three stories high, to really do it justice. You familiar with the chicken scene in *Texas Chainsaw Massacre*?"

"Don't know the chicken scene, no."

"Well, I won't tell you, then. Just spoil it for you."

"I think I'll go up and look in the windows," I said.

"Go ahead. You got my permission, and I'm the only one around."

This wasn't true for long, though. I was looking through a ground-floor window at a large, empty room when a voice said, "Just you hold it right there, buddy."

I felt myself jerk a little, the way you do when somebody catches you where you oughtn't to be. A thick-necked, crew-cut young man had come around the corner. He wore a powder blue uniform shirt and pants of the same wrinkle-free fabric, with a black stripe down them. A stainless-steel pin on his breast pocket said "SSS." Instead of a tie, the man wore a pale yellow scarf, ascot-style. He also wore a wide pistol belt, with an empty holster. The pistol was in his hand. He looked and sounded frightened.

"Hey, hey," I said. "Easy does it."

"Just you hold it, I told you," the man said. "And don't you come no closer, neither."

I was afraid he might shoot me to cover up that he wasn't the kind of guy he was always reading about in *Soldier of Fortune* magazine after all, but was just scared. I was scared, too, and didn't mind if it showed in my voice. I wanted him to think he was safely in control, which is where all cops and cop wannabes are happiest at being.

"Listen, I'm sorry," I said. "I heard the place was for sale and I thought I'd take a peek." If I were any good at ingratiating smiles I would have tried one, but they don't come naturally to me.

"Yeah, sure, asshole like you's going to buy this property?" he said. "Tell me about it." Once again, I had failed to look like a millionaire. But at least Bubba here felt he was back in command enough so he could rely on elegant insult instead of shooting.

"Hey, officer," Pennington said from behind me. "How you doing?"

"Stand right where you are," the guard said, moving so that he could cover both of us. "This is private property."

"Well, hell, I know that. I'm Jim Bill Pennington."

He didn't look any more like a millionaire than I did, not to me. But he was somehow giving off the right Texas recognition signals to the guard, who put his gun back in his holster. "I got my orders," he said.

"You did just right," Pennington said. "You know old Lonetree? George Lonetree?"

"Don't believe I do."

"Might have been before your time. He was a lieutenant with SSS, used to kind of keep an eye out when the Somervilles had people over. Now look, if you ever see this sorry son of a bitch hanging around again, I don't want you to mess with him. Just shoot him down like a dog. Only thing they understand, these Yankees."

Now the guard was smiling. He even fastened his holster strap. "I'll do that little thing, Mr. Pennington," he said.

"Factory rejects like that," Jim Bill said as we headed back across the lawn, "sometimes they can break bad on you."

"I figured. I was exposing my soft parts to him when you came up, but of course pulling rank is even better."

"What can I say? I'm an honorary admiral in the Texas navy."

"Is there really a Lieutenant Lonetree?"

"Sure. Would I lie to the troops?"

"What the hell is the SSS?"

"It was Denton's little toy army. Called it the Sunbelt Security Service. He got into a whole lot of weird sidelines before his empire collapsed and fell. A funeral parlor, couple of nursing homes, medical labs. He even bought a twelve-story building near the Medical Center and made it over into suites the family could rent while daddy was down the street dying. Sunbelt Security was what he set up to guard all that stuff, plus the real estate he controlled all over the place. I'm surprised his little army didn't dry up and blow away along with everything else. I guess a few bubbas like that one stayed on the payroll to guard the wreckage."

"Whose payroll?"

"Good question. The receivers? I don't know. Maybe SSS was making money and stayed afloat somehow."

The guard made a gesture as we pulled away, something between a wave and a salute. I waved back and got up to what I figured was speed for a subdivision.

"Hey, slow down," Pennington said. "No, even more. That's it. Just crawl along. Drives these assholes crazy when tourists come through and rubberneck."

A Saab blew its horn once and then pulled out. As it passed us, the two women in the front seat looked at us in what sure enough seemed to be an unfriendly way. Pennington tossed his empty out the window, and I watched it in the rearview, clanking end over end along the gutter. "Live in these goddamned houses to show off to each other," Pennington said. "But they get all torqued out of shape when the common folk come around to gawk." He reached back and fished another can out of the sack. "Want me to crack one for you?"

"I'll wait," I said. I was thinking about the Somervilles, sitting in that big house night after night. "You suppose she ever beat him at gin rummy?"

"Billene? He might have let her beat him sometimes. Make her feel good."

"There you go. He had a soft spot after all."

"Yeah, he did. About the only good thing you could say about the son of a bitch was how much he loved her. Apart from that, no redeeming social value at all."

"The papers said he was charming."

"You never know what people mean by that, do you? What they're liable to mean is what I mean when I say he was smooth as owlshit. What a psychiatrist would call a sociopath. He could be cold like a snake, or friendly, or shouting mad, depending which would work best for him at any particular time. He'd look you right in the eye and lie to you if that was the best way to get whatever he happened to want. Or he'd tell the truth, either one. He didn't give a shit which. Hey, whatever worked.

"People weren't really people to him. They were just obstacles or stepping-stones. That's why some folks might have said he was charming. He could act charming if it suited him, and acting was good enough for most of the people he dealt with. They wouldn't know real charming if it came up and pissed in their boot. Let old Denton sling an arm around some sucker's neck and lower his voice a little like they had secrets from the rest of the world, just the two of them, and most times the poor asshole would feel warm all over. Like if the Duke of Windsor had somehow taken a shine to him, and he couldn't figure why, but it sure felt good. Right up to when he got home and found his wallet was cleaned out. Right down to that old rubber he used to keep in there in case he ever got lucky."

We were getting out of the high-rent neighborhood by now, so I edged my speed up to twenty-five or so. "Where to?" I asked Pennington.

"Let's go to your motel and drink some beer, then. I go home, all I'm going to get is a big, economy-sized ration of shit from my wife for drinking in the afternoon. You don't drink, do you?"

"I'm drinking."

"Yeah, but you don't drink."

"I used to."

"And one day you just decided to cut down? Then you didn't really drink."

"Try puking in every gutter in Fairbanks. Try losing jobs, losing your wife, your kid."

"Okay, you drank. And now you have two beers while I'm having six. You know how unusual that is? Most guys have to quit all the way."

"I thought about it, but I figured that would be admitting the booze was in charge. I wanted to be in charge of the booze."

"Never work for me, I'll tell you. Shit, I know who's in charge."

"Well, different strokes."

"So let's pull in here and get some cold."

My motel was more of an inn than a motel. A two-story wing off to one side had rooms that opened to the outdoors, but the main building had three stories, corridors, elevators, a lobby, a lounge that seemed to be closed all the time, banquet rooms, and a restaurant. The big signboard out front read WELCOME SCHLOSSERS OF AMERICA.

"What the hell's a schlosser?" Pennington asked.

"People. If your name's Schlosser, you get to go to this convention every year if you want to. Last year it was in Kansas City, I heard."

"I should have known. Penningtons have the same goddamned thing. One year it was in Fort Worth and I figured what the fuck, I might as well go. Bad move. I should have thought the thing through. What kind of people have such an exciting life that they'd travel halfway across the country to spend three days in a Ramada Inn with a bunch of strangers that have the same last name?"

"These Schlossers are okay. They've got a Schlosser song they sing before dinner."

"Jesus, let's get up to your room fast. You can't hear the song from there, can you?"

Pennington had scored for a couple more six-packs along the way, so I iced them down in the sink with the four warm singles left over from the first batch.

"What'd you think of Miranda?" he called in from the

bedroom. I popped one of the cold ones to keep him company, and went back out to him.

"I don't think I'd want her on my case," I said.

"You got that right."

"She said her father was disbarred. What's that all about?"

"Bribing jurors for Humble Oil. She idolized him and she never forgave him for it. Been throwing him in jail over and over again, ever since she got out of law school. Those poor sons of bitches she prosecutes, they don't have the slightest idea they're all her daddy."

"How about Humble Oil? She ever get back at them?"

"Oh, she'll take a crack at the big corporations whenever she can. But that's not too often these days, with the Republicans running the Justice Department."

"She got to go after the S and Ls, though."

"Yeah, but they're not really corporations even though legally they are. Not big bureaucracies like Humble Oil. The S and Ls are more like individual con men dressed up as corporations. I love these thieving sons of bitches. Every night I go down on my knees and thank Reagan for turning them loose on us."

"How come?"

"American history is my field, and swindlers are my field of specialization. Fisk, Gould, Mizner, Ponzi, Teapot Dome. I did my thesis on the Yazoo land frauds." The professor paused to take a good hit of the beer while it was still cold.

"Well, Jesus," he went on, "one morning I come downstairs and find that Santa left Ronald Reagan under the tree for me. The whole goddamned government is suddenly a criminal conspiracy. The Reagan-Bush administration has been a swindle on a scale the robber barons couldn't begin to conceive. There's never been more money looted from the public in the history of the world than the Reagan-Bush gang has done in the last ten years. Can you imagine what it's been like for a historian with my particular specialty?"

I nodded. My idea of how to find things out is to keep people talking, no matter what about, and sort it all out later.

"Well, it's been hog heaven. It's like I was a military historian with a specialty in the Napoleonic Wars, and I pick up the papers one morning and find France and England are fighting the Battle of Waterloo all over again. Exactly the same, only ten times bigger. And I can follow it day by day. I even know Napoleon and the Duke of Wellington. I mean, I used to play tennis with Baker when I was a kid. I remember seeing Bush around the Bayou Club, when I'd hang out there with my rich cousins. A lot of the biggest thieves are up in New York and out in California, but a lot of them are right down here in Houston, too. Hell, I grew up with a lot of them. Hog fucking *heaven!*"

"Any of these guys I should talk to?" I said. "About Somerville, I mean."

"P.J. Potter, I guess."

"Who's he? Oh, wait a minute. Is that the partner, Dr. Paul Potter?"

"That's him, P.J. He's your basic fat, jolly bubba, only don't let him fool you. He'll cut your balls off if you don't watch 'em, even if he's not a damned urologist like Denton was. A lot of people that did business with old Denton, there's something they forgot to ask themselves. What kind of guy looks over the whole medical school catalog and then decides to spend the rest of his life whacking up other guys' dicks?"

"What kind of a doctor is Potter?"

"A cardiologist."

"So that's what he went back to after Sunbanc blew up?"

"He never really left it, although he did take in a young associate to do most of the work. Even now, P.J. only sees a few old patients. Rest of the time he manages what's left of Denton's empire."

"How much is that?"

"Probably a lot by our standards, but chicken feed by the standards of major bottom-feeders like Denton. I don't know for sure, but my impression is that P.J. mostly manages the dough that Denton squirreled away in his wife's name. On the other hand, the only way that impression would get around is from P.J., I guess. So who knows? Maybe P.J. stole the whole damned pile himself, and stashed it in the Cayman Islands."

"You think Potter would talk to me?"

"Why not? He's not ashamed of anything. None of these guys are. They blame everybody but themselves for the collapse of the S and L industry. Everything would have been all right if the government had stayed off the backs of guys like them and Keating."

"I'll give him a call," I said. "All he can say is no."

"If he does, you can always talk to Judge Metcalf."

Again I knew the name from the newspaper clippings I had read, but it took me a minute to drag it up. "Theodore Metcalf," I said. "The black federal district court judge who recused himself from Somerville's case because they were friends. Didn't he later . . ."

"Yeah, he did. Resigned from the bench when it turned out Denton had cut him in on some basically smelly deals. Now he does poverty law out of some rat hole on Dart Street. I bet he'd just love to tell you about his old pal."

"They were pals, him and Somerville?"

"Probably what the judge thought by the time Somerville was finished putting the moves on him. You have to get pretty tight with a federal judge before you can put his balls in your pocket."

"That's where Metcalf's balls were?"

"That's where Somerville thought they were, only the judge took 'em back finally. Go talk to him, ask him."

I went to grab us both another beer. Pennington was still ahead of me, two for one, but he didn't seem any the worse for wear. Real lushes build up immunity, the way you can to rattlesnake venom. I used to be able to function pretty well myself, carrying a load that would paralyze most social drinkers. Paralyze me, too, these days.

"I'm surprised Miranda didn't mention Judge Metcalf," Pennington said. "The judge had a good reputation all his life, and she blamed Dr. Denton for corrupting him. Because of her own daddy doing what he did, a briber is what she hates the most. She doesn't see the larger picture, poor old Miranda. Putting the fix in is only a minor element of the big store game. You know what the big store is?"

It turned out that Pennington's studies had got him interested in confidence games as well, and that the big store was an innovation that somebody named Ben Marks hit on in 1867, in Cheyenne. Basically you set up what looked like a legitimate business and staffed it with con men. "It'd be a phony Western Union office, maybe. Or a whole damned brokerage office complete with a stock ticker, only everybody in it would be working for the head grifter. Customers, secretaries, brokers, everybody except the mark. That's what these S and Ls were, and we're starting to find out that's what our biggest banks and insurance companies are, too. All a bunch of big stores. The mark comes back the next day once he

figures out he's been swindled, and there's nothing there
but the bare walls.

"If you knew the history, you couldn't read the business pages for the past ten years without laughing out
loud. You'd think all these half-bright greed-heads had
thought up $E = mc^2$ all by themselves, but every single
thing they came up with was just another old-time scam
with a new name. You take the leveraged buy-out, for
example, that that asshole Bill Simon was so proud of.
The Mafia's been doing the exact same thing to small
businesses since the turn of the century, only they call
it a bust-out.

"It was like old times, seeing the classic swindles
come back to life during the eighties. Reagan turned out
the lights at the regulatory agencies, and every piece of
shit all over America started to sprout mushrooms. All
of the old frauds and cons popped up again, but the
main one was the Ponzi game. You pay yesterday's
depositors impossible interest rates out of the money
you take in from today's depositors, and everything is
swell as long as new suckers keep bringing their savings
in.

"Same underlying theory as a chain letter. Normally
anybody with the brains of a doorknob throws out a
chain letter, of course. But suppose you got one that
said the federal government will reimburse you up to a
hundred thousand dollars for anything you send to the
people behind you in the chain? Then suppose you call
up your congressman and he says, Yeah, that's right, the
U.S. Treasury guarantees it. Well, now you go fish that
letter out of the wastebasket, don't you? Now you want
to keep that chain going. And the ones who started those
chains were people like Denton Somerville. They were
never the last fool."

"Last fool?"

"That's what the S and L thieves called it. Go back to the chain letter. Every fool in the chain makes money—except for the last fool. In this case, of course, the Federal Deposit Insurance Corporation was the last fool. Which means you are."

The professor got himself another beer from the bathroom, and when he came back his thoughts were on yuppie cattlemen.

"What do yuppie cattlemen have to do with it?" I asked.

"It's the last-fool principle in biological terms," Pennington said. "You take some thirty-five, forty-year-old accountant or lawyer or broker, some goddamn thing, and he's got a blond wife and one-point-eight blond kids and a shiny new four-by and a ten-acre spread seventy miles out of town where he takes the family every weekend and the kids hate to go on account of there's nobody to play with so they take a couple of their friends along from school, okay? Well, by now the only thing that sumbitch doesn't have is cattle. How's he going to tell the folks back in New Jersey he's in the cattle business on the side? Can he just buy a cow and tie it up to the porch? He's not exactly sure, but he thinks you can't just feed them on the weekends.

"So what he does, he goes to the annual high-society cattle auction and gets drunk along with every other yuppie in Houston, and when he walks out of there his wife's pissed at him because he just got through buying a fancy pedigreed cow for eighty thousand dollars. It wasn't like he was picking his nose, either, and the auctioneer thought it was a bid. No, this damn idiot of hers *meant* to do it.

"Now, he can't keep the eighty-thousand-dollar cow out to the place, so he's got to pay even more money to board it with the auctioneer. Can't eat an eighty-thousand-dollar cow either, he's smart enough to figure that out. In fact the only thing you can do with it is get eighty-thousand-dollar calves from it, but the cow is worth too damned much to risk knocking her up. So you hire a vet and he takes his shirt off and shoves his bare arm up to the shoulder into old bossie's cunt and he flushes her egg right out and gives it a shot of jizzum from some two-hundred-thousand-dollar bull and then he sticks that egg up some retired milk cow so she can be Mary Beth Whitehead.

"The idea is, the vet's going to flush bossie out like that over and over again, and each time you got you another eighty-thousand-dollar calf, are you following this with me? Are you seeing the mathematical flaw here? What you got is a finite number of yuppie fools with eighty-thousand bucks, and that finite number is smaller than the number of bossie eggs that their cows are pumping out . . ."

We were reaching the point of diminishing returns, and Professor Pennington seemed to think so, too. When he finished about the cows, he said he better get on back home. That's another sign of the experienced drunk. He knows when it's time to hang it up.

As I drove him back to where his car was parked, he told me about Yellow Kid Weil, Charley Gondorff, Slobbering Bob, the Postal Kid, and various other con men who had preceded Dr. Denton Somerville to that Big Store in the Sky.

"They're all together now," Pennington said. "Swindling the shit out of one another and waiting for the Ronzo to come along and tell them how in the hell he managed to blow off two hundred fifty million suckers all at once."

He looked steady walking toward the car, and I figured he'd probably make it home just fine, slow and careful.

Go to bed early, feel pretty good tomorrow morning, and be ready to lecture at nine. I also figured it would probably be a damned good lecture, certainly better than most of the ones I've sat through. But then Rice is a better school than Harvard. One day in Cambridge I got to talking with a kid who had transferred up from Rice. He said his professors there had warned him that the quality of the teaching would be lower at Harvard, that he'd see less of his teachers, that the grading would be easier, and that the work wouldn't be nearly as hard. All this had turned out to be true, the kid said. In fact it was why he had transferred. He wanted more free time for extracurricular activities.

5

NEXT MORNING I WAS AT the Federal Building when it opened, to get the address of Harmon H. Harmon, Denton Somerville's former chauffeur, from the deposition I had skimmed earlier. Harmon lived in a place called Highlands, or at least he had when the government lawyers questioned him. The clerk told me Highlands was twenty miles or so east of Houston. He also told me where to find the probate court. There I looked up Denton Somerville's will. It was pretty simple. After the payment of his funeral expenses and "just" debts, all the "rest, residue, and remainder of the property of which I shall die seized or possessed or to which I may in any way be entitled at the time of my death or at a future date or dates, both real and personal, of whatsoever kind or character and wheresoever situated, I give, devise, and bequeath to my wife, BILLENE SOMERVILLE." The executor was PAUL J. POTTER, M.D.

I called Dr. Potter from a pay phone in the lobby and naturally failed to reach him. You can get through to the pope faster than you can get an American doctor on the phone. "To what is it in reference to?" asked the woman who kept him safe from patients.

To the late Dr. Somerville, I said, representing myself as Tom Henderson representing the *Boston Globe*.

"Is that the name of your company, sir?"

"Sort of. It's a newspaper. In Boston."

"What is the nature of your complaint, Mr. Henderson?"

"I don't have any complaint."

"Then this is not in reference to a medical matter?"

"No, it's in reference to a newspaper story. I was hoping to talk to . . ." And so on. After hearing me out, she said Doctor was busy. She said she would pass the message on to Doctor, although she didn't sound hopeful about my chances for an audience. She sounded as if Doctor was booked straight on through till the turn of the century.

I had better luck when I called Theodore Metcalf, the former federal judge. He answered his own phone and gave me directions to his office on Dart Street. I left my car in the parking lot near the courthouse and walked, for the pure pleasure of walking without a coat, in the warm sunlight. Dart Street wasn't far, but even a ten-minute walk gave me an idea of what it would feel like to be an alien. Once I left the courthouse area, I never saw another pedestrian. Naturally nobody had thought of building sidewalks for my species, so I kept switching back and forth between gutter and roadside, depending on which was less cluttered with litter evacuated out of its windows by the dominant life form.

Metcalf's office was in a stucco bungalow that needed paint. A couple of old-fashioned iron lawn chairs sat empty on the porch. They needed paint, too. The sign out by the street was too new to need paint. It read SAN JACINTO LEGAL CLINIC. Under that, smaller letters said FIRST CONSULTATION FREE.

I went in through a screen door on a spring. I knew enough to catch it behind me so it wouldn't slam; we had the same kind of door on our house when I was a kid. Over to the left of what had been the bungalow's living room was a yellow oak desk, the kind with a shelf that swings up from a recess for the typewriter to sit on. The typewriter was an IBM Selectric, newer than the desk but not by much. The middle-aged black woman working on a letter said, "Mr. Henderson?"

I nodded after only an instant's hesitation. I was getting pretty good at my new name.

"The judge is expecting you. He'll be off the phone in a minute."

"I'm off the phone now," a bass voice said behind me. I turned and saw a tall, heavy man silhouetted in his office door. "Come on in, Mr. Henderson. Bring us in some coffee, would you, Lucille?"

"Mrs. Pluckett won't quit calling me judge," Metcalf said, waving me to a chair and taking one himself. "I've given up telling her not to."

"Why fight the tide?" I said. "Everybody in Washington that ever held a Schedule C job goes by 'Mr. Secretary' the rest of his life."

"True, but these last few years I've learned the value of fighting the tide. Should have learned it a lot earlier."

"Meaning before you ran into Denton Somerville?"

"Meaning that, yes. Why would your paper still be interested in Somerville at this late date?"

"The money aspect. People read that this S and L stuff is going to cost us five hundred billion over the next forty years and it means nothing. It's like how far is it to Mars? Too far to make any sense of. But how about the individual operators who made millions? A reader can get a handle on a million dollars. Just the interest would pay his salary for a couple of years, minimum. How much of that dough stuck to these guys? Where did they hide it? The Charles Keatings and the Don Dixons, how much did they personally walk away with?"

"I can see the interest in those fellows, all right. But why Somerville? He's dead."

"Exactly."

"Can't sue?"

"Partly that. Partly it adds to the story. As stories, Keating and Dixon will just dribble on through the courts, jails, whatever. The way Jack Kennedy would have dribbled on through retirement if he hadn't got shot. But when Kennedy died his story turned into a mystery everybody loves to read about. Because we don't know how it would have ended."

Metcalf nodded, as if this made sense to him. I hoped it did; I had even gone so far as to set down for myself a list of reasons why my editors might be interested in a dead swindler. And this was part of what I came up with.

"Well, I don't know how much Somerville might have made off with," Metcalf said. "But I'm sure it ended up with Billene. The usual ploy is to put all you can into a trust fund in your wife's name. That way the government can't get to it, but you maintain effective control of it."

"If she lets you, anyway."

"I doubt if Denton worried about that. Billene would have jumped off of the Transco Tower if he said to."

"Was that because she's stupid or because she loved him?"

"A little of both. She certainly loved him, and vice versa. And she was certainly stupid, at least in the sense of I.Q.'s or·SAT scores. But folks with skin the color of mine don't do too well on those tests either, and I'm not ready to say that means we're dumber than you white folks.''

"Us white folks didn't do very well on those tests, either, at least not the ones I grew up with.''

"Where was that?''

"Kind of a rural slum in upstate New York.''

"You made it out, looks like.''

"I was a jock.''

"That sometimes helps, doesn't it? Anyhow, to get back to your question, Billene had a kind of emotional shrewdness sometimes. I remember her seeing this certain young girl across the room and saying poor little so-and-so, just look at her. She's putting on weight like a feedlot calf. She must be doing that so somebody will let her alone. A couple months later the girl's mother filed for divorce, and it came out that the father had been molesting her.

"Now, I used to sit in juvenile court many years ago when I started out on the bench, and I know overeating is a pretty complicated thing, medically and psychologically both. But I don't remember that it's particularly a sign that a child is being sexually abused. And here Billene spotted it right off, even though she barely knew the family. If a psychiatrist made that kind of an intuitive leap we'd call him pretty damned smart, wouldn't we?''

"Probably we would, yes.''

"I used to look at Billene and I'd think how there wasn't that much difference between her type of Dixie belle and an old-time black Uncle Tom. Both of them having to get along with Massa, both of them doing it just perfectly. Billene was inside her husband's skin. She'd know what Denton wanted before he did, and she'd want it for him harder than he did. If he hated somebody, she'd hate him too, and so he'd hate the person in question all the more, and then she would, too, and so forth. They kind of brought out the worst in each other that way.

"Was that dumb, though? On her part? Or was it smart, the same way the Uncle Tom has to be smart? What's smart? You tell me."

"Sounds to me like you already know," I said. "Do you think she'd be smart enough to handle all that money she wound up with?"

"Smart enough to find somebody who could."

"Like this Dr. Potter?"

"Exactly like him, I expect."

"Did she move on to him after Somerville died?"

"Not if you mean as a lover. Billene might possibly get over Denton someday, but not in just a couple of years. No, she's off on the *Billene,* being a widow."

"On the Billene?"

"Denton named their yacht after her."

"She lives on it?"

"Far as I know she does."

"Where's it docked?"

"Used to be the Waterford Harbor Yacht Club. Now I couldn't say. If she's been back to Houston since the funeral, I haven't heard of it."

"Where did she go?"

"Off sailing is all I know. P.J. Potter could probably tell you if he wanted to."

"He'd be the one she'd call for money?"

"That would be my guess. I haven't actually spoken to P.J. for some little time now. After all, he did his best to ruin me."

"How's that?"

"By publicizing information about my business dealings with Dr. Somerville."

"Both the Post and the Chronicle gave the impression that their information came from Somerville himself, not long before he died."

"Yes, that's the impression they gave. But look back at those stories and you'll find that they don't actually say it straight out. My own information is that P.J. was also a source. Maybe the principal source. Although of course he planted the material on Denton Somerville's orders."

"Those stories confused me," I said. "Well, I guess what confused me wasn't the stories, but why you resigned after they came out. If the deals you got from Somerville were supposed to be a bribe, seems like the bribe didn't work very well."

"Is this what you're interested in writing about?" Metcalf said. He didn't sound hostile, just curious.

"I wondered, that's all. It could be off-the-record, if you want."

"I had a law clerk once who was a reporter for a news service before he went to law school. What he would say is that if you don't want to see it in The New York Times, then don't say it. That's the only off-the-record there is, according to him."

"Probably good advice," I said.

"So make it on the record," the judge said, to my surprise. "Even if it isn't what you're writing about, I hope you can work it in."

"That wasn't a bribe?" I asked, puzzled about where he was going.

"Whatever your readers conclude," Metcalf said. "I just want to get my story out to as many people as possible. About all I'm good for anymore is to be a horrible example."

"You want me to dredge up all those stories about your dealings with Somerville, and your resignation?"

"If you can work it in, yes. Let me try to explain it to you. President Carter appointed me to the federal bench. I let him down. I let my profession down. I let my people down. Now I could do like Marion Barry and the rest of them do, say the white folks are picking on me. But that's not the point. The point is I did it, guilty as charged. Just me. Doesn't matter if there's a double standard, either. I knew there was, known it since I first asked my mother how come we were black and other people were white. I should have met both standards. So should every other black in public office. That's what I want to say, every time I have a chance to say it."

Naturally this made me feel pretty good about wasting his time, but I went right on doing it anyway. "Okay," I said, "but what are you guilty *of*? Maybe you got money, but you didn't do anything for it."

"That's not the point, either. The point is taking it in the first place. The Bible says, 'Thou shalt take no gift; for the gift blindeth the wise and perverteth the words of the righteous.' You don't have to do anything in exchange for the gift. It blindeth and perverteth anyway.'

"That's the Bible," I said. "How about the law?"

"The law says pretty much the same thing, where judges are concerned. I could have ridden out those stories and probably stayed on the bench. Only Congress can impeach a federal judge, and it almost never does. But that isn't the point either. The point isn't whether you can beat the rap, it's whether you're guilty. I decided I was, and I sentenced myself."

"If you don't mind my asking, how did you get in the whole mess in the first place? Somehow, you don't seem like the type."

"I didn't think I was, either. So why don't you write

about the process of corrupting someone who isn't the type? It might make the next person smarter than I was."

"What is the process?"

"It starts with rationalization, like all sin. The corrupter understands that. He helps you along. He's just your friend at first, and you're flattered. You're a public servant. You're not rich. He is. This is because there's injustice in the world. The work you do is just as important as his. In fact, it's a lot more important. In a just world, your services to society would be worth as much as his. More. He slips this into the conversation now and then, not often. You don't say anything, but you agree inside. It's what you always thought yourself, actually.

"You drive an Olds, he drives one of his Jaguars. You fly commercial, he has his own plane and pilot. You book an economy cruise, he has a yacht. You go to the movies. He has his own personal theater. Well, these are just toys, he says. Not often, you understand. Just drops it into the conversation somewhere and passes on to the next thing. He knows he doesn't deserve toys like that. In fact a big part of his pleasure from them is to share them with people who do deserve them. He's going on a little trip next week, in fact, and there's room. Why don't you come along? Play a little golf in Arizona, catch some trout in Idaho.

"He never asks for anything. Now and then maybe he says something about how awful it is that the country has its values so mixed up, millions for some people and nothing for the people that really contribute. Teachers, preachers, politicians. Judges, too, now that he thinks of it. Maybe he mentions how lucky he is, how he has more than any man needs or should have.

"After a while it turns out now and then that he isn't along himself for those trips on the private jet. You happen to say you're going to Denver for a conference, and it turns out he's sending the plane up that way empty, just about that time, to pick up some people. Why don't you hitch a ride? No sense wasting the seat. Might as well toss your skis on board and have some fun in Aspen while you're out there, the condo's just sitting there empty. What the hell, you think to yourself, why not?"

"And if a guy says he's making a pickup in Denver," I said, "it wouldn't be polite to ask him who he happened to be picking up at the same time you happened to be going there . . ."

"No, that would be nosy."

"Ungrateful."

"Suspicious and unfriendly," Metcalf agreed. "All the things that I should have been when my old friend and I were sitting in his lovely living room in his lovely River Oaks home one night, drinking fine whiskey and looking at the logs crackling in the fire . . ."

"The fire?" A cold day in Houston was when you only had to change shirts twice.

"Denton liked having a fire. Said it reminded him of New England. The butler would light the fire, then turn the air conditioner up."

"The way Nixon used to have them do in the White House?" I said. "Kind of a Republican energy program?"

"Maybe," the judge said. "So anyway, we're sitting there in front of the fire and Denton says he knows how concerned I am about underrepresentation of blacks in the bar, and he's been wondering what a private citizen could do about a problem like that. What would I think of a nonprofit foundation to look for solutions? Good, good, he's glad to hear me say that. Because he's just this week set up exactly such a thing. Would I consider doing a kind of prospectus for it? Setting out an agenda?

Just a few pages would be plenty. Quality, not quantity. So I wrote it.

"A month or two later a check comes for twenty-five thousand dollars, which works out to about ten dollars a word. Naturally I can't accept it. Denton is crushed. My contribution to the success of the project was worth a lot more than that, God knows. It never occurred to him that there'd be a problem. He couldn't be sorrier. Just tear up the check, of course.

"Meanwhile it's getting kind of expensive to keep up with the Joneses. You can't let your new buddy and his buddies pay every tab. You hate to be the only one in the crowd that isn't picking up his fair share. Particularly if you're black, if you follow me."

"I think I do."

"So with a little bit here and a little bit there, it adds up. The kids have to go to St. John's all of a sudden. Everybody else goes there. Two kids, it costs just about a quarter of my gross income. Fortunately a guy on Denton's S and L board is on the board of St. John's, too, so there's scholarship money. They're bright kids, pretty good marks. They deserve it. See how it goes?"

"I see."

"Even with that, though, you're spending more than you're making. Not that you don't deserve it. Hell, you waited tables to make it through Howard, didn't you? Pumped gas to make it through night school and get your law degree. Still, it comes in handy when Denton lets you in on a real estate investment trust with no money down. It's a sure thing, and you can pay your share into the trust out of the profits. Just what happens, too. You make forty-five thousand dollars, you pay the trust back twenty-five thousand dollars, and you've still got twenty thousand dollars left. Perfectly legal. Perfectly honest. The next deal is an even bigger one, and this time you net sixty-two thousand dollars."

I was remembering what Jim Bill Pennington had told me about the way the roper played the mark in the classic confidence games. I could see what was coming, and it did.

"Third time the real estate market is drying up, and the deal goes sour. I wind up owing the trust one hundred and fifty thousand dollars, only this time there's no profits to pay it out of. No problem, says my pal Denton. This is small change to him and the other guys in the trust. The market's going to firm up again and he'll put me into something that'll make me whole again. Meanwhile, don't worry about a thing. You've got more important things to do, Ted."

Ex-Judge Theodore Metcalf looked at me with what almost managed to be a smile. "See where he's got me by now?" he asked.

"He's got you hammered into a crack."

"It doesn't feel like a crack, though. Nobody ever says another word about one hundred and fifty thousand dollars, even when Denton and Sunbanc are going down in flames. It's like the whole thing never happened."

"Only you signed papers, and somewhere it's all down in black and white."

"That part didn't seem important at the time, though. Maybe they forgot it, you know? We're talking about a collapse up there in the billion-dollar range. Maybe those few dollars I owed just fell through the cracks. I was actually beginning to think something like that had really happened."

"Wouldn't he have needed to call in every debt he was owed, by that time?"

"You'd think so. That made me feel guilty, too. What if he *had* forgotten, and now he really needed every penny he could get? But still, what good could my few pennies do, when he owed thousands of times that much? I couldn't save him. Paying off would ruin me, without helping him. Besides, the lawyers would wind up with most of it anyway. Besides, he had gotten me into this mess in the first place. Besides, the son of a bitch had turned out to be a crook anyway."

Judge Metcalf smiled again, or maybe it was more of a sneer, at himself.

"Oh, the human mind is a wonderful thing," he said.

"Way back then, what was the purpose of getting you indebted to him?" I asked. "Somerville was riding high when he first cut you in. He couldn't possibly have known that he'd get in trouble years later. Let alone that his case would be assigned to you."

"I was only one out of many, although I wasn't bright enough to see it at the time. I felt it was to Denton's credit that he didn't spend all his time with other businessmen, that he had so many politicians and other government types among his friends. But of course that's a big part of the business these guys are in, corrupting state power for their own ends."

"Or trying to, in this case," I said. "When it came right down to it, you refused to be bribed."

"That's right. Denton's investment was about to pay off after all those years, and I recused myself. Said I wouldn't take the case because of my personal relationship with him. And that's why I'm sitting here today, instead of in my old courtroom that I worked my entire life to get to."

"Because you did the right thing?"

"Because I did the wrong thing, twice. From the point of view of legal ethics, I took a bribe. From Denton's ethical point of view, I didn't deliver on it."

"So he leaked your dealings to the papers as pure payback?"

"Absolutely pure. I never saw that vengeful side of him before, but then he wouldn't show it to me, would he? Since Sunbanc collapsed, though, people aren't scared anymore, and they've started to come forward. Even more so since he died, of course. It's become pretty obvious that Denton was capable of practically any cruelty if he was crossed."

"Or even if he wasn't," I said.

"How do you mean?"

"Selling those worthless bonds in his umbrella company when he knew they weren't backed by anything, especially not the FDIC. Christ, he apparently sold them to his own chauffeur."

"Poor Harmon. That was amazing, even by Denton's standards. Denton figured I had betrayed him, so he took revenge on me for just the pure pleasure of it. Understandable, maybe. But imagine cheating poor Harmon! 'Old Harmon here, he'd eat broken glass for me, wouldn't you, Harmon?' Denton used to say. And Harmon would look embarrassed and say, 'Yes, sir, I reckon I would at that.' "

"What about P.J. Potter?" I asked. "Would he have eaten broken glass for Somerville?"

"He might say he would."

"But he'd be lying?"

"Not exactly, but it was different. They were in a lot of ventures together, so their interests were pretty much the same. What was good for Denton was likely to be good for P.J., too. But P.J. wouldn't have followed Denton off a cliff. In fact, he didn't. They made a lot of money together, but P.J. wasn't named in any of the indictments. And P.J. seems to have kept hold of his share of the money."

"Maybe Somerville kept hold of his money, too. By switching it all over to his wife, the way you said. Or putting it overseas where she could get at it."

"Maybe," Judge Metcalf said. "Or maybe it isn't an accident that P.J. stayed out of trouble with the law and managed to hold on to so much money."

"How do you mean?"

"I've often wondered if Denton wasn't setting P.J. up as his equivalent of an offshore bank. Siphoning money off from the main operation into P.J.'s pockets. But P.J. would really just be parking it for Denton, the guy who was taking all the risks."

"To do that, he'd have to trust P.J. a lot, wouldn't he?"

"That's a problem, all right. But maybe he did trust him a lot. After all, he trusted P.J. to handle Billene's affairs. I think it's even in the will."

"It is. He's the executor."

"I wouldn't let P.J. be my executor."

"Why's that?"

"Because I think he's every bit as big a thief as Denton was. A lot of people have been fooled by that bumbling, simple-minded good-old-boy stuff of his. The impressive thing is that a lot of them were people who use the same act themselves."

"So what's to stop him stealing the widow blind?"

"Not a thing in the world. In fact I suspect that's exactly what he's doing, except I can't prove it and you can't print it."

"Not unless Dr. Potter himself tells it to me, I guess."

"Lots of luck."

6

THE GROUND-FLOOR LOBBY of the Dunn Tower didn't have a desk that I could see, but otherwise it was along the lines of any other lobby in any other incredibly expensive hotel. Just after I walked in, three gray stretch limos pulled up at the entry. Doormen opened the passenger doors. Out from behind the smoked windows came a fat-cheeked warrior of the desert, carrying about two hundred pounds on a five-foot-five frame. He wore a pale gray suit that had no doubt been made by the best tailors money could hire, but there's only so much you can do with a lard tub.

This particular lard tub was an alpha male. You could tell it from the swarm of service troops around the cars: porters pushing huge brass luggage carts, a collection of suits from the front office, women wearing veils and floor-length robes who were getting out of the limos, the kids they carried or held by the hand, the two body-guards, the man who was interpreting into Arabic what the suits were saying in Texan. Maybe the butterball was a prince or a king. Some kind of major thief, anyway, come to Houston to do a little shopping.

Except that a couple of the suits wore stethoscopes around their necks. And that the statue in the middle of the lobby wasn't Conrad Hilton. It was Dr. Michael E. De Bakey. I watched until the emir, or whatever he was, disappeared into the elevators along with his retinue. And then I wandered past expensive shops and restaurants on the mezzanine for a while. I was in no hurry. One time was as good as another to drop in on Dr. P.J. Potter, since I didn't have an appointment. When I got around to asking, his office turned out to be across the street, in a building called Scurlock Tower. I hadn't bothered to call ahead because I figured it would be harder to refuse me face-to-face than over the phone. And I couldn't see much reason for Somerville's partner in crime to want to see me. But you never know till you ask, as I should have realized from watching all those crooks committing suicide for Mike Wallace on "60 Minutes." P.J. Potter turned out to be glad to see me.

His middle-aged receptionist had just got through telling me that Doctor saw patients by appointment only, and then only long-time patients, as he was cutting down his practice, when Doctor himself came through the door.

"Hey, Louise," he called out, "how they hanging?"

"Oh, Doctor," she simpered. Outside of old movies, it was the first time I ever heard a woman simper.

"Hey," Dr. Potter said, this time to me, "how you?"

"Just fine," I said, "I'm—"

But the doctor charged right ahead before I could start lying about who I was. "What can I do you for?" he said. "I reckon Louise told you I'm not seeing new patients, but I can send you to a guy pretty near as good as I am. Come on in and tell me what's wrong with you, podner."

I followed him along inside his office before telling him there was nothing wrong with me. I figured he'd listen me out at least, once we got sitting down. And he did.

"Damn, all the way from Boston!" he said when I was done. "You got a press pass? I always wanted to see me one of them."

I handed him the laminated pass that would allow the bearer, Thomas G. Henderson, to cross Boston police lines unless the cop who inspected it happened to know what a real press pass looked like. Potter scaled the card back to me and swung a couple of lizard-skin cowboy boots onto his desk. He was a big, thick-necked man, who looked like he might have played defensive tackle somewhere. He wore a string tie with a turquoise clasp and a class ring with a blue stone in it. I couldn't read the name of the college, but the medical school diploma on the wall was from the University of Texas. Another framed document said he was a member of the American College of Cardiologists or whatever. Potter's face was permanently set in a slight smile, and it broadened often into a great, big smile. Very friendly fellow.

"You know old Terry O'Rourke up there?" he asked.

"In Boston?"

"At your paper."

"No, I guess I don't. It's a pretty big place."

"You seen his name on stories, though?"

I thought a moment. I skim the *Globe* every day and I couldn't recall seeing his name, no. "Not that I remember," I said.

"Well, maybe he's on some other paper. Y'all got another paper up there?"

"The *Herald*, yeah."

"Probably that's it, then. Well, you go ahead and tell me what you want to know about old Denton and I'll help you all I can. I'd like for somebody to tell the truth about him, for once."

"What is the truth?"

"The truth is that Denton Somerville was the kind of damn visionary that made America great. He was a whole lot more than just another businessman. What old Denton really was, he was a great social engineer who just happened to make his living in the savings and loan industry."

"The Justice Department—" I began.

"Justice! You shitting me? Those assholes over there don't know no more about justice than a hog knows about Sunday. That goddamned Miranda Weeks, I had an old-maid teacher in second grade looked just like her. All she needs is about eight inches of stiff dick to straighten her out, and won't nobody give it to her. You ever seen that skinny old gal? A man stuck it to her, he'd hit bone."

I nodded, although the fact was that he was exaggerating by a little bit.

"It wasn't nothing but a goddamned vendetta," Dr. Potter went on. "Vendetta against the whole savings and loan industry, and poor old Denton just got caught up in it. If the government had kept its goddamned nose out of something it didn't understand, we would have grown out of the whole goddamned thing.

"Them goddamned pointy-headed bureaucrats don't know nothing about dreams, and Denton didn't know nothing but. That's what he was, Denton, a dreamer. And he could make 'em come true, too, don't think he couldn't. I seen him do it a hundred times. I tell you something, this city looks a whole lot different today because of Denton and maybe another handful of men like him. But he was the best of them all. Pure and simple, he was the best."

"I heard Mrs. Somerville had pretty near as good a head for business as he did," I said, even though I never heard any such thing. Probably Dr. Potter hadn't either, because he laughed.

"*Billene?*" he said. "She handled the other end. The spending, not the getting."

Getting and spending, we lay waste our powers. Not too many doctors, let alone good old boys, know Wordsworth. Just in time I stepped on the impulse to ask him what that "getting and spending" stuff was a quote from. Let him think I was just a good old boy, too, Yankee division.

"I guess she can't do too much spending anymore," I said instead.

"Oh, she does right well still. Not as well as before, but Billene ain't hurting one bit."

"You're the executor, aren't you?"

The doctor broke into a big, friendly smile. "You really been doing your homework," he said. "I swear, that's something I could never do, be a reporter. I don't know how you fellas come up with stuff the way you do."

"I just went down to the court and looked at the will, is all."

"I be damned. It's simple once you think of it, idnit? Yeah, I'm the one gives Billene her allowance."

"I would have thought the whole estate would be eaten up by creditors and lawyers."

"You sure got that right."

"What would the allowance come out of, then?"

"Denton put stuff in her name all along. There's plenty to keep her going."

"If it's in her name, what would she need an executor for?"

"Well, I maybe shouldn't have said allowance. That was just a manner of speaking. What it is, she has me manage her affairs for her. What she had when Denton died, plus what I managed to save out of the wreckage."

"Like the house?"

"No, that was Billene's in her own name. But the god-damned bureaucrats didn't pluck us all the way clean. One or two little old pieces of property here and there, a medical lab, one or two holes in the ground . . ."

"Oil wells?"

"Not to amount to much, though. You know what they call an oil well, don't you?"

"What?"

"A hole in the ground surrounded on all sides by liars."

"Are you selling the wells?"

"Why would we sell them? They ain't exactly Spindletop, but there's oil in them."

"I thought maybe you were selling everything off for her, since the house was on the market."

"Damn, you really *have* done your homework."

"I went out to have a look, till the guard chased me off."

"Hell, I'll tell him to show you around inside, if you want to. Who was it, Roy? Kid with a crew cut?"

"Sounds like him. He work for you?"

"Indirectly he does. That's another thing we held on to. Denton set up Sunbelt Security back when he had hundreds of properties to guard. Now the damned government's got them, but we still got the contract to provide security. Turned out to be a pretty good little business, tell you the truth. We got us an ex-FBI agent who's just smart enough to run it right and not quite smart enough to steal it out from under us."

"Us being you and Mrs. Somerville?"

The doctor nodded.

"Where does she live, now that the house is up for sale?"

"On her boat. She said that's where her and Denton were happiest, and that's where she's going to stay the rest of her life. She took his death awful hard. A doctor sees a lot of that, but I never saw a woman carry on like Billene did. She was in his bedroom when he died, you know."

"I thought he died in the hospital."

"Well, he did, but it was up on Fondren twelve. Up top of the Fondren Building is where we've got the VIP suites. You're a sheik or something, you can bring your whole harem with you. Wall-to-wall carpeting. Living rooms where you can serve tea to your visitors. TV monitors in the halls for security. Art originals on the wall. Those damned antique chairs you don't dare to sit on for fear they'll break. Man can bring his own pajamas and bedding. Order his meals from a gourmet menu. Only way you can tell you're in a hospital is the beds crank up. Old Billene had her own bedroom, right next to his. She just stepped away from his bed to take a leak or some goddamned thing and when she come back in there was Denton, all cranked up in bed and watching TV just the way she left him, only he up and died on her during 'Guiding Light.' "

"Just like that, huh?"

"Well, it wasn't hardly a surprise. How we first got together, me and Denton, was he had a history of cardiac episodes, and he came to me with chest pains, oh, I don't know, more than ten years ago. Over the years he had a bunch of minor attacks. In fact the reason he was in the hospital was because he just had another one three days before.

"So you could say it wasn't sudden, but it sure shocked the shit out of Billene. I was just coming to look in on Denton, and I heard her screaming all the way down the hall. She wouldn't let go of his hand even when the nursing service took him down to the morgue. I had to go along with the gurney because she wouldn't let loose of him. Finally I managed to get some Seconal into her down in the morgue, calmed her down enough so she'd let the funeral home people take the body away.

"I kept her sedated right through the funeral, and thank God she held together till the services were over. But right after, she took to her bed for six weeks. Just locked herself up in the house all alone, wouldn't see anybody, wouldn't answer the phone. One morning she called me, real early. I just got out of the shower, matter of fact. Said she was going to live the rest of her life all alone on her boat."

"Is that possible?"

"Why not?"

"Don't you need a crew for those big yachts?"

"Hell, they pretty much run themselves. Probably she could have made out all right. Her and Denton both knew what they were doing around a boat. But you're right, it'd be a stretch for a woman alone. I told her that. Told her she better let me get somebody to help her out."

"Just one man?"

"All you need. I got Sunbelt Security to find a good hand for her."

"Why Sunbelt Security?"

"A boat isn't all that safe a place for a woman alone. I wanted somebody who could kind of look after her, too."

"Sort of a bodyguard?"

"Sort of. It's a big ocean. Lot of people loose on it that you wouldn't want to be alone with."

"How about him?"

"Who, Glen?"

"If that's his name. The sailor. Isn't it a little risky to let her go to sea with just him?"

"Lonely widow type of shit, you mean?"

"That, too. But what I was thinking, there wouldn't be much to stop him from grabbing everything in sight and taking off."

"That's another reason why I hired him through Sun-belt, so's he'd know she wasn't alone and defenseless with him. That there was a bunch of mean sons of bitches back here that was holding him responsible."

"Smart enough to run the boat but not smart enough to steal it from her?"

"Now you got it."

"Mean enough to protect her but not mean enough . . ."

"Oh, old Glen ain't that bad."

"Still, a boat with just the two of them, day in and day out. It could get pretty crowded."

"I told her to let me know if she wasn't comfortable with him and I'd get somebody else. But so far it's worked out good."

"Meaning she's comfortable with him?"

"Meaning just exactly that and not one thing more. I told Glen about that in no uncertain terms. You're not there to hold the pretty widow's hand, what I told him. You try that, mister, and your ass is grass. And I'm the lawnmower."

"Probably someday she'll want her hand held, won't she?" I said. "You got to get on with things sooner or later."

"Probably someday she will," Potter said. "She can't spend her whole life on that boat."

"Where does she go in it?"

"Mostly she's just been sailing up and down the East Coast, sometimes over to the Bahamas or the Virgin Islands. She hasn't set foot back in Houston since she left."

"How does she handle business stuff?"

"Oh, we talk by phone every week or so. I doubt she'll ever be back, now that she's selling the house. Get that in your story, Tom. Get it in about that poor, ruined widow woman that those sorry bastards in Washington turned into some kind of Flying Dutchman."

"I guess I don't follow you," I said. "What bastards?"

"Goddamned regulators that murdered her husband, simple as that. Man that did as much for this city as the Cullens or the Joneses or the Hermanns or any of them. Denton's heart probably would have held out another twenty years, hadn't been for all the goddamned persecution they put him through. I tell you, I blame that goddamned Bush for not calling the dogs off of him. Bush lived here long enough to know better than to act thataway. What the hell's the point of having a president that calls himself a Texan if the sorry son of a bitch won't look out for his own kind of people?"

"Not just his own kind of people," I contributed. "Won't even look out for his own family."

"Well, that's right," Dr. Potter said. "Didn't even look out for poor old Neil, that didn't do a thing but sit on the Silverado board. I'd like to know just what the hell's wrong with sitting on the board of a savings institution."

I went through my number about how interested my editors were in where all the money wound up when giant financial institutions collapsed, and P.J. Potter smiled and kept saying things like, "Know just what you mean," as I went along.

At the end I said, "What I'm trying to sort out is who are the winners, if there are any. And who are the losers."

"You looking for the losers," Dr. Potter said, "you looking right at one. Me and old Denton himself, I guess we were the big losers."

Aside from the taxpayers and the thousands of people like my old men back in Cambridge, I thought. And like Sally under the bridge in San Diego, asking Somerville for mercy but not quite crazy enough yet to bother sending the letter.

"The winners, I guess you mainly got the lawyers. Them and the big bottom-feeders like old Jim Fail. You know about him, don't you?"

I nodded. Fail had put up a thousand dollars of his own money, borrowed $70 million more, and the feds in charge of the S&L bailout sold him fifteen thrifts that proceeded to pump something like $20 million a month into his pockets. He was one of dozens of multi-millionaires—Ronald Perelman of Revlon and Caroline Hunt, the daughter of H. L. Hunt, were a couple of others—who were allowed to paw through the wreckage and pick out the good stuff. The way the bailout operates, the government keeps all the S&L's bad loans and sells billionaires the good ones at a fraction of their real value. It's the Republican version of workfare.

"That's what you ought to be doing your story about," Potter said. "There's a bunch of regulators wound up rich in that Jim Fail deal and all the others, too. I'll bet you a dime to a dollar on that."

"Okay, then," I said. "The lawyers and the bottom-feeders and maybe some crooked regulators, all of them were winners. Who else? Mrs. Somerville was a winner, too, I guess."

"I don't see how a man could say that," Dr. Potter said. "That woman is destroyed, damned emotional wreck is all she is. Wandering around on her boat. Only thing keeps her going is pills."

"I meant financially a winner."

"Not even that. If Denton had died before all the shit come down on him from Washington, she'd have been a whole lot richer than she is now. You got to look at it in proportion. In proportion, she took as big a hit as me or Denton. I'm not saying she's not comfortable off, you understand. Just saying in proportion."

After a little more of this, I was beginning to develop a sympathy for reporters. Potter was running on and on, friendly as could be, but not really saying anything. He couldn't estimate what Mrs. Somerville was worth because the bean counters and the lawyers handled all that, he didn't know where or whether Denton Somerville had parked any money before his death, he didn't even know where Mrs. Somerville was exactly, although most likely it was on the eastern seaboard somewhere. On and on.

When I finally gave up, Potter walked me to the outer office, a heavy arm laid over my shoulders. He was telling me how much he admired reporters, how he himself took a journalism course once from a famous former newspaperman and was almost going to be one himself till he decided on medical school instead, and on and on and on.

"Oh, listen," he said in the outer office. "I almost forgot. Louise here ... Look at her, ain't she a pretty little thing? I like to keep young stuff around the office ..."

"Oh, Doctor, you're just *terrible*."

"Anyway, you just give this young lady a number

where she can reach you and she'll set it up for you to visit Denton's house any old time you want. And I'll call you if anything more comes to me that you ought to know."

It didn't seem likely to me that anything would, but I gave Louise the motel number anyway. Actually, I was curious to see the inside of the mansion. And maybe to talk some more with the guard, who would presumably be a little more friendly when I came recommended. He might have been on the job back when the Somervilles were still in residence. He might have seen something that would turn out to be useful, although I couldn't think what.

From the Houston Medical Center, I headed out of town on the Gulf Freeway, and then past the Lyndon B. Johnson Space Center toward the yacht club that Billene and Denton used to sail out of.

The Waterford Yacht Club was right off Galveston Bay. There was no gate, and so I drove right in. My Datsun looked definitely downscale among the other cars parked there. But I looked upscale, in my cotton seersucker jacket, open-necked blue oxford shirt, light gray slacks, and cordovan loafers. Most of the other men in sight wore polo shirts or T-shirts, with khaki or denim trousers.

As I headed down toward the boat slips I saw a sign that read "HARBOR MASTER." Behind the counter was a college-age kid with no shirt, rolled-up white duck pants, and bare, brown feet. "Sure, I remember Miz Billene," he said. "I helped get *Billene*, I mean the boat *Billene*, not the lady, I helped get her ready when she took off. I reckon she still considers this her home port, but she hasn't been back since. Maybe never will, I wouldn't be surprised. 'There's nothing but bad memories here for me, Tommy,' she told me, day she left . . . no, I don't know for sure where she is now. You might try old P.J. Potter on that. My guess, though, she's probably following the spring . . . Where? Well, I don't know for certain, but I'd bet a lot she's heading up toward Maine. She likes to get up there right around the end of April, beginning of May, before the crowds . . . yeah, I do, as a matter of fact, on account of a couple other members take their boats up there later on, in the real season. She goes to a place called Islesboro."

I let the boy get back to whatever he was supposed to be doing and walked down the hill to where the boats were. A man carrying a cooler out to his launch was ready enough to set it down on the dock and talk to me. Maybe the *Houston Post* had actually been right about God installing extra-big hearts in Texans. They were more hospitable than Bostonians, at least. Everybody I met had been willing, one way or another, to set their coolers down and talk a while with a stranger.

When this Texan learned I was a landlubber, he told me what a boat was. "It's a hole in the water surrounded by wood into which you throw money," he said. A sort of an oil well in reverse, I gathered. He had known Billene and Denton both, so he said, and confirmed that she was likely to be gunkholing her way toward Maine about this time of year. Gunkholing, he explained, was putting in at one little port after another, seldom getting too far from land.

"Is sailing like flying?" I said. "Do you have to file some kind of a flight plan with the Coast Guard or somebody?"

"Nah, it's more like driving around with a house trailer. You just take off and go. Nobody in the world has a clue where you are unless you let them know.

Maybe you're famous for fifteen minutes after you
anchor, with everybody asking where you came from
and how was the crossing, like that. But that's about it.
You could give 'em any name you wanted at the marina,
and wouldn't nobody know any different. Or care. The
way marinas work it, if you got the money, honey, they
got the time."

"So if you wanted to find somebody who was off sailing, there wouldn't be any way to locate them?"

"Not unless a man'd get lucky."

Which I had already done back in the harbor master's
office, provided the kid was right. Felicia Lamport, the
poet and a one-time teacher of mine at night school, had
a summer place on Islesboro. I had never been there, but
I knew it was a small island off the coast of Maine near
Camden. I remembered Felicia saying that the local eti-
quette was for drivers to wave at all oncoming cars. It
didn't sound like the kind of place where it would be
hard to find somebody.

Back at the motel or hotel, whichever it was, the
Schlossers of America were getting ready to hang it up
for another year. It was the evening of the annual fare-
well banquet. Noisy Schlossers were all over the place,
having a great old time. I wished I were a Schlosser, or
a Trump or a Reagan or even Alfred E. Neuman himself.
The unexamined life is the only one worth living.

I was getting ready to hang it up myself. The trip had
let me see Hope again, and the sun again, and I hadn't
really counted on much more than that. Treasure doesn't
come in chests anymore. Once money gets into banks
and computer terminals and brokerages, it's pretty hard
to get the stuff out again.

All I could figure to do was to try and find Harmon
H. Harmon tomorrow on my way out of town. If he

didn't know where any treasure chests were, I'd go back and tell the old men in Cambridge that I had flunked out. Meanwhile, I might as well start packing for an early departure next morning. So that's what I was doing when a knock came on the door.

"Yeah?" I hollered.

"Verily," a man outside the door answered. Or Sherri Lee. Or something. He knocked again, a good deal harder than was polite. I went over by the door, pissed off.

"What the hell do you want?" I said.

This time the voice said, "Security," so I opened the door. A man came in just like he had business there, without asking. He was the opposite of those guys who cover up their bald spots by combing long hair over them. This guy camouflaged his by a variant of the Yul Brynner ploy—wearing what little hair he had in a short, blond, bristly crew cut. He was a couple of inches short of six feet. He had a sinewy build just starting to thicken up a little. The look of a cop or a drill sergeant or an astronaut, about ready to retire after twenty years in.

"All right, mister," he said, "let's start out with just who the hell you really are."

I didn't say anything, just looked at him. Whatever he was, it wasn't hotel security. His summer-weight suit was a slick, shiny Italian number that probably cost him six or eight hundred dollars. Personally, I'd rather wear a Nehru jacket.

"You heard me," he said. "Who the hell are you and what are you up to?"

"Tell you what," I said. "Fuck you."

"You'll regret that, mister."

I sat down on the bed, leaned back against the headboard, and clasped my hands behind my neck.

"Tell you what else," I said. "You hustle your ass out of my room right now and I won't whip it for you."

The man pulled a short-barreled revolver, the kind detectives carry, out from under his suit jacket.

"Oh, please," I said.

He put the revolver back in its holster and said, "Just so you know where we stand, fella."

He had some kind of southern accent, but I couldn't place it. There are hundreds of southern accents, sometimes different from one little town to the next. All I could tell was that he wasn't Texan, because I had been hearing enough of that lately to know. I kept quiet, feet stretched out on the bed and hands behind my head, so as to let him come to me. He produced a leather folder and held it open to show official I.D. When I swung my feet to the floor to go take a closer look, he flapped the folder shut and put it back into his shirt pocket.

"It says FBI," he said.

"Why would the FBI be interested in me?"

"You tell me."

"Actually, I can't think of any reason at all."

"Look, you're wasting my time here. There's nobody by the name of Thomas G. Henderson that works for the *Boston Globe*."

"Oh, yeah? Did you ask them?"

"That's none of your concern. Hey, what the hell do you think you're doing there?"

"I'm opening this phone book here. Then I'm going to look in the blue pages for the FBI, and give them a call. See if they sent somebody around to talk to me."

"I didn't identify myself as an FBI agent."

"Yeah, I noticed that."

"I went into private industry after I left the bureau."

"Wow."

"Mister, you come down here and try to worm stuff out of people using a phony name, you're looking for real trouble."

"And you're just the boy to give it to me, huh? Tell me something, do you feel like you're losing control here?"

"Just what's that supposed to mean?"

"Means you expected me to piss down my leg when you showed me your great big wonderful gun and your great big wonderful card with FBI on it, only my pants are still dry. So you feel like you're losing control, so that makes you talk tough."

"Fuck you, asshole."

"See?"

He pulled out his gun again, and this time he aimed it right at me. Intellectually, I knew he wasn't going to shoot me. Emotionally, I was scared. But naturally I tried not to show it. That's the Code of the West.

"You'll answer me, asshole, or you'll wish you did," he said. "Now let's see some real I.D."

"I left it home."

"Where's that?"

"Saranac Lake, New York." One of my brothers worked as a prison guard there.

"What are you doing down here?"

"Working on a story about your old boss."

"I got no boss."

"Don't you work for Sunbelt Security Services? Dr. Potter said it was still part of the Somerville estate."

"It is, and I'm the president of it."

"Of the estate?"

"I'm getting tired of your wise shit. You don't work for any newspaper. What are you really doing here?"

"I'm just a researcher, really."

"Only thing you're researching is robbing Miz Billene or kidnapping her, one or the other. Come down here with phony papers, asking all kinds of questions about where the Sunbanc money went, who's got it, how'd they get it, where are they exactly. You wouldn't be trying this shit on all by yourself. Who are you working with?"

"I'm like you, whoever you are. What'd you say your name was?"

"E. R. Hostetter is who I am."

"Well, Mr. Hostetter, like I say, I'm like you. Got no boss, not working with anybody. I could, though. Let me try you out on something. Suppose you came here to talk to me tonight just like Dr. Potter told you to. Only I just checked out and you missed me. You with me so far? Then suppose later on that a particular person actually does get robbed or kidnapped.

"You see what I'm getting at here? If I knew some of the answers to those questions I've been asking around town, then the person who gave me those answers would be as good as a partner to me, except nobody would know we had ever even met. It might be a pretty good piece of business. Might even put you in a position where you could buy Sunbelt Security and really be your own boss. You want to give that some thought?"

For a moment he did, for a long enough moment so that I knew he was for sale. Unfortunately, it was also long enough for him to figure out that he might have a lot of trouble finding me to collect.

"You're disgusting, you know that?" he said. "Takes a real low kind of a man to go around robbing widows. Let me tell you something, if anything happens to that poor woman I'll make it my business to get to you before the police do. And I guaranfuckingtee you there won't be anything left of you to arrest. You got my personal word on it, and I never broke it yet."

He waved his gun at me.

"Let's have your wallet," he said.

"I don't carry one."

"Then empty out your pockets and toss everything over here to me."

All I was carrying was money, a comb, a handkerchief, a penknife, the car keys, my phony press pass, and my phony business cards. "Where's your driver's license?" Hostetter asked.

"I don't have one."

"Bullshit. Shove that briefcase over to me."

That was where my license was, sure enough. It didn't say Tom Bethany on it, but it did say Tom Carpenter and it did give the address of my apartment in Cambridge. I had full documentation for Tom Carpenter, which was the name my neighbors and the Department of Motor Vehicles knew me by. It wasn't a name or an address that I wanted Hostetter to have, though.

"I keep my license in the glove compartment," I said.

"Let's go get it."

I got up, him moving back as I did so. Hostetter was keeping three or four steps from me at all times, as if we were two magnets with the same polarity. I wasn't at all sure I could cover the distance fast enough to disarm him. On the other hand, I was pretty sure he wouldn't be crazy enough to fire at me in a hotel room anyway, with God knows who in the corridor outside. I wasn't nearly so sure that he wouldn't risk it in the parking lot, though. I didn't know anything about him, really. Whether he was sane or nuts, reckless or cautious, or what kind of jobs he was used to doing for Potter, Somerville & Co. My best plan might be just to walk away from him in the lobby.

"I'll be right behind you going out," Hostetter said. "Try any shit on me and I'll aim for your spine. While everybody's trying to figure out what the noise was I'll be walking out. Anybody's in the parking lot, it won't matter. I put my plates in the trunk before I drove in."

I had the bad feeling that I wasn't the first person he had taken through a public place at gunpoint.

We went down the stairs together, and out through the lobby together. "Which one's yours?" Hostetter asked.

"The Datsun over there, with the Massachusetts plates."

"That's what you drive? That fucking junker?"

I had already spotted what had to be his car, a new Tempo with no plate on the rear, sure enough. It bothered me a lot that he had taken that plate off before he came to the motel. I was trying to remember, to get back into my bones, a combination of moves that I used to practice with one of the CIA case officers in Long Cheng. Part of it was a disarming technique he had learned in hand-to-hand combat training, and part of it was standard wrestling stuff. We'd do it more or less drunk in the Sky Bar, with the little black beer-drinking bears in their cages down below the windows. We'd swap turns with a cocked and empty .45, trying to beat the click when the hammer went down. Because I was faster, mostly it wound up that I would have shot him and he wouldn't have shot me. I had no idea how fast Hostetter was.

We were over by my Datsun now. I was going for the keys to get inside when I remembered what both of us had forgotten, that the car keys were still on the bed in my room along with all my other pocket junk. "Oh, for God's sake," I said, "you know what we . . ." And I spun.

I had his hand. I heard and felt his wrist break. While I was still leaning into him, I heard the gun clunk on the ground. When I let him go to kick it under the car, he bolted. But by the time he ran behind a small building back of the motel pool, I was so close that I would have had him in another couple of steps. Running, he looked back at me just long enough to miss seeing a raised three-inch drain pipe that came out of the little building. It clothes-lined him right at the ankles, and his head smacked the concrete pavement with the sound of a medicine ball hitting the floor.

I tripped over the pipe, too, only I went into an instinctive tuck that landed me safely on top of Hostetter. He never moved. I got up and looked out from behind the little pumphouse or whatever it was. Nobody. I went back to Hostetter and bent over to listen. He was breathing, sort of, but it was harsh and shallow. It sounded very bad. I took a moment to think about the spot I was in. It was time for Thomas G. Henderson to disappear, fast. To slow down whoever might try to follow him, I emptied Hostetter's pockets into mine. Then I left him there, hoping he'd stay unconscious for a while. Or even forever. If he wanted me to feel sorry for him, he shouldn't have brought the gun along.

Back in my room, I finished packing. The job only took a few minutes, since most of it had been done before Hostetter barged in on me. I checked the yellow pages for a safe place to hole up in, and then called the desk downstairs. They told me they were very sorry but weekly rentals were not refundable and I couldn't get my money back for tonight even though my plans had changed and I had to leave right away. It was the answer I expected, but I didn't want the room clerk to wonder why I was carrying luggage past her when my week wasn't up yet.

Once the car was loaded, I went back to the rear of the pool house to check on Hostetter. He still lay there like a corpse, but he was still making the same awful breathing sounds, a death rattle over and over again. I left him and went back to the parking area out front. Pretty soon a man and a woman came out. "Excuse me, sir," I said, "but are you staying here in the hotel?"

"Huh? Oh, yeah. Yeah, we are."

"Well, the thing is, there's a man lying out behind the pool house, real sick. Unconscious. Looks like he had an accident. Seems like somebody ought to tell the hotel people about it."

"There's a woman behind the desk you could tell."

"Well, you see, I'm not even supposed to be here. If it got in the papers I was at some motel and my wife found out . . ."

"Where is this guy?"

I pointed the way and watched the man go off, with the woman trailing a few safe steps behind. I fished Hostetter's gun out from under my car and drove sedately out of the parking lot. When I was halfway down the block I turned my lights on. When I was around the corner on Kirby Road I pulled over, got out the map, and figured out how to get to Highlands. There was a campground in Highlands, I had learned from the yellow pages, and campgrounds are just about as good as a yacht if you want to play hard to find. Cops might go through the list of hotels and motels if they're under real pressure to find somebody, but you'd have to shoot the president before they'd bother running a tent check out in the boonies.

And Highlands was not only safe. It was handy, too. The last person on my list to see lived out there—Harmon H. Harmon, Dr. Somerville's old driver.

7

CAR DOORS AND KIDS' VOICES woke me at the campground early the next morning. Some overachiever was moving out at dawn, I thought until I looked at my watch. It was coming up on eight o'clock, although the light filtering through the tent was so weak it seemed much earlier. I poked my head out and found the sky overcast. But rain didn't seem to be threatening, so there was no need to strike the tent and pack it away just yet. Instead I used the light to have another look through the stuff I had cleaned out of Hostetter's pockets. The folder he had let me look at from a distance held a card that said FBI, all right, but the full quote was "National Association of Former FBI Special Agents." He was also a member of various other associations of investigators and law enforcement officers. The eighty-four dollars in his wallet were now in my shirt pocket. The rest was pretty much the usual: credit cards, business cards, driver's license, Blue Cross/Blue Shield, and so forth. The only out-of-the-way thing was a pistol permit, which I figured I'd mail to my post office box in Cambridge. Maybe I would make up a bunch of pistol permits with my Macintosh. I couldn't think of any real use for them; it just seemed like a good idea at the time.

Hostetter had carried a fancy notebook, the kind they call executive planners. Global time zones, overseas area codes, metric conversion tables, each working day subdivided into little half-hour planning blocks from nine to five, all of it designed to give the owner the sense that he is master of time, space, and the universe in general. Hostetter had used it, just like everybody else probably did, for notes and addresses and phone numbers. He could have used a regular dollar-nineteen spiral notebook for the same thing, but of course it wouldn't have had the genuine Moroccan leather burgundy binding with the American Express logo stamped on it in 14-karat gold leaf.

On yesterday's space, Hostetter had written one or two reminders that didn't mean anything to me, and then a couple that did: "BG 617-929-2000 no record. 994-2121. SW mot inn buff. 10K?" This had to mean he had called the *Boston Globe*, where they never heard of any Thomas G. Henderson. Then he called the number I had left with Dr. Potter's receptionist, discovered that it belonged to the Southwest Motor Inn, and asked for directions. They told him to get off the freeway at the Buffalo Speedway exit. The "10K?" wasn't so straightforward. As a fee for finding out what I was up to, it seemed pretty excessive. As a fee for killing me, it could have been the going rate in Houston for all I knew. Did the question mark mean the price was tentative, or still open for negotiation? Or that it was still undecided whether to do the job, whatever the job was? I didn't have enough information to know the answer. But none of the implications seemed pleasant, and the size of the price tag seemed way out of proportion to the offense of impersonating a reporter.

I remembered a high school teammate who was our best defensive guard even though he was so nearsighted that everything beyond arm's length was a blur. The way he managed to make tackles was by reading the pressure on him. If the blockers were trying to move him left, he would drive to the right until a ball carrier appeared out of the haze. The ball carrier appearing out of my own haze was starting to look like Billene Somerville.

Highlands, once I had a chance to drive through it in the daylight, turned out to be a collection of one- or two-story buildings scattered along a few miles of a road that ran north off I-10 about twenty miles out of Houston. A sign said the population was 7,500, although the town didn't look nearly that big. Another sign, outside a juke joint called Frankie's Place, said HARLEY PARKING ONLY.

Like Houston, Highlands didn't seem to have neighborhoods with separate identities. An RV park might be next to a bank. A beat-up trailer home with trash in the yard might be next to a neatly kept brick suburban, or a large, white-columned house. The dominant architectural form, though, was the one-story wooden bungalow, ten years past due for a paint job and sitting up off the ground on cinder blocks.

I found a place for breakfast and got directions to Harmon H. Harmon's house along with the check. "You can't miss it, it's a big old white school bus. He won't have no trouble finding it, will he, Homer?" the waitress said to the short-order cook.

"Hell, no," Homer said. "You just go down that road she told you till you come to the first white school bus on your left, and that'll be it."

"There ain't but one white school bus down there, Homer," the waitress said.

"Jesus, Ellie," Homer said. "That's the whole point of the joke."

The road led me past a dump, and then down into a muddy bayou with dead cypress stumps sticking up out of the gray muck. The gray-brown mud flats were threaded with a maze of channels a foot or two wide but only a fraction of an inch deep.

The place looked about right for a chore I had to do, and so I pulled off the deserted road and got out. A squadron of little shorebirds was marching along in loose formation, stopping now and then to probe the mud two or three times with their long beaks, then moving on to do the same thing over again a few feet farther on, all pecking pretty much in unison. Life its own self.

The sky was light gray and featureless. An egret stood out white against it, sliding down through the air at full flaps till it disappeared into the tangled swamp on the other side of the mud flats. A half-dozen ducks floated over by the swamp, where the water was deeper. High-tension wires crossed the whole scene, bellying between enormous towers and disappearing into the swamp.

The raised roadway split the bay of mud in two. The sloping banks of the ramp were jumbled with riprap made of busted slabs of concrete, the rusted reinforcing rods twisting out of them. The muddy banks were slowly swallowing up plastic tubs, cans, chunks of Styrofoam, bedsprings, and an old car seat next to a sign warning of an underground petroleum pipeline. The weeds and cattails and the mud were the permanent elements, though, as they went indifferently about the slow business of returning this industrial wasteland to wilderness. They could make a few more artifacts disappear with no trouble, and so I tossed Hostetter's gun into the gumbo. It made a heavy plop, then sat on the surface for an instant before beginning to slowly disappear. The wallet and the executive planner might not sink as well, though, so I poked them down into the muck with a stick. Like the little shorebirds, only in reverse.

A little bit down the road I drove past a burned-out trailer with insulation hanging out from its buckled walls. A swing made of a tire hung from a live oak. It had been there so long that the tire had sagged from its own weight into the shape of an egg hanging from its narrow end. The abandoned trailer was the nearest thing to a residence I had come across since leaving the muddy bayou, and I was starting to wonder if I had the right road. Then around a turn, sure enough, I came across a white school bus.

Rust showed through where the white paint had powdered off. A narrow robin's egg blue line ran along the side of the old bus, as out of place as racing stripes on a dumpster. The bus still sat on its tires, not on blocks, although it seemed like the tires should have gone flat years ago. Now, in March, the weeds that grew around the bus were already waist high; by summer they'd probably be up to the bottoms of the windows.

The windows were amazing, bits and patches of glowing colors like the stained glass in some crazy cathedral. Seams of black separated the colors, like a network of scars. The colors made no picture or pattern, and the patches were of random sizes. Ellie back at the café had been right. You couldn't miss it.

I had to step across a drainage ditch to get from the road to where the bus stood. There was an iridescent sheen on the brown water. When the hot weather came, the whole area would smell of crude oil and marsh gas, as the earth slowly leaked and then redigested itself. I figured I was in Harmon's territory once I had crossed over the ditch, and so I hollered out to announce myself. When nobody answered, I went around the bus to the side where the door was and hollered again. This time an enormously fat man came to the door, and I wondered irrationally if I had come to the wrong place. For some reason I hadn't been thinking of Harmon H. Harmon as fat.

"You come to the right man," he said when I explained what I wanted. "Ain't nobody knew the doctor the way I did. Knew him before his wife did, even."

"Just what I was hoping," I said.

"I'm in the middle of something, but you come on in and set. I can talk while I'm doing it."

The smell hit me like a wall when I went up the school bus steps. It had to be an oven inside there most of the year, and Harmon was a long way from any shower, or any water that wasn't even dirtier than him. But if the odor didn't bother him, it probably wouldn't bother me after a few minutes. Any more than the moldy smell in cheap motels.

"Want some pop?" Harmon asked. "Only thing is, it's warm. Ain't got the electricity out here."

"No thanks."

"Got Ahrasee Cola," he said, giving RC the local pronunciation. "Coke, Slice, Diet Sprite?"

"I'm not thirsty, thanks," I said, even though I was. But I'd rather drink muddy water than any of those things. My body is a temple, at least to that extent.

"Well, sit down, then," Harmon said. "Tell me what a poor man can do for you."

He lowered himself into a chair with the caution of a man who's had chairs collapse under him. It was a sturdy armchair, upholstered in a crazy quilt of fabrics. The visitor's chair was an aluminum lawn chair, with a half-dozen or more different colors of webbing, all crisscrossing to make a pattern of clashing squares. The webbing was taut and the aluminum frame had been rubbed to a shine. The armrests had been taken down to bare wood and refinished with polyurethane. Harmon's own chair, now that I took notice, had been carefully worked over, too. The little wooden legs seemed freshly painted with high-gloss enamel. One was green, one was red, one was blue, and one was yellow. The patches that made up the upholstery were neatly sewn. Harmon was sort of neat, too; he just smelled. He wore one-piece fatigues, the kind the army used to issue to motor pool mechanics. Two mechanics could have fit inside the pair Harmon had managed to find for himself. The fatigues were patched at the points of wear: elbows, knees, and seat. Like all the other patches, these were of varied colors. Harmon saw me looking.

"You happen to notice that dump on the way in?" he said. "Saturdays I help out there, and the boss lets me pick every day. A man can live good out of a dump That's where I get all my material from."

He pointed to his clothes and armchair, and to a mattress and box spring sitting on a platform made of stacked railroad ties. The ties were planed smooth and set with dozens and dozens of shiny pieces from tin cans he had cut into crescents, stars, and other shapes. The decorations were held in place with screws, nails, and tacks of all types and sizes. The bed was covered with a spread made entirely of bits of Day-Glo fabrics in more colors than I thought Day-Glo came in.

"Impressive," I said, which it damned sure was. Now that I could see the inside of the windows, the stained-glass effect came from scraps of colored plastic or cellophane held to the glass with seams of black electrician's tape. The whole inside of the bus was alive with the colors that glowed through the windows and fell onto the colors already inside.

"I use bottles and jars and stuff for the windows," Harmon said. "They got some nice color to them. Look around the supermarket someday and you'll see how pretty the colors are. For these here decorations on the bed I use tin cans. You clean up a tin can good and keep it dry, it's never going to rust on you. It's when the damp gets to them they get all nasty."

He had picked up the tin can he must have been working on when I came, and got busy with an old kitchen knife, scraping off the little patches of glue that had held the label on. On a plywood workbench beside him were tin snips, pliers, odds and ends of wire, hammers, punches, and all sorts of other tools. Dozens of small jars held screws, nails, brads, tacks, nuts and bolts.

"Not a thing here but what it come from the dump," Harmon said. "Folks don't believe that when I tell them. Take a look at that block plane there. You believe a man would throw a good block plane away? Well, somebody done it. They'll throw anything away."

There was so much crammed in and jumbled and piled all over, hanging from the ceiling, loading down shelves, jammed under things, that it took a good, long look to see just what Harmon H. Harmon had built for himself. It was a sculpture for him to live in, like the shell of a whelk. All around him he had built dozens of gaudy abstract constructions out of junk, all bathed in the light show created by his windows. I picked up a small piece made out of sardine cans, plastic beads, copper wire, and aluminum foil, and then set it down again. Harmon got halfway up out of his chair, moved the piece a couple of inches, and sat down again with the sigh that a fat man makes settling back down where he belongs.

"Don't go where you set it," he said.

"Sorry."

"Ain't your fault. Ain't nobody but me knows where everything goes. People say Harmon you old fool, don't make no difference where you set things. But it does. I made everything for the exact spot it's in."

And this was so, I could see when he had pointed it out. When I was wrestling for the University of Iowa I took an art appreciation course that was supposed to be easy enough for us jocks to handle. The professor told us about a retarded boy who spent all day drawing little pictures on a big piece of paper, and then drawing frames around them. The boy had never heard of the golden rule of proportions, but his horizons and so forth would always wind up within a fraction of an inch of where they were supposed to be. Harmon had that same kind of natural eye, or at least everything in the place looked to me as if it fit together just right. It was the same with each of his constructions or sculptures or inventions or whatever they were. They seemed to be clutter put together at random, but take one piece of tin or plastic or wire off them and they wouldn't look right anymore. On the other hand, what do I know? I only got a B− in the course.

"How long did you work for Dr. Somerville?" I asked.

"More than ten years," Harmon said. He kept on working at the tin can, which looked small in his huge hands. His hands moved carefully. I suspected he was one of those men who can take apart a transmission and hardly get their hands dirty. "I was having trouble pissing, and at the hospital they said go see this fella Somerville so I done it. Damned good thing, too, or I'd be dead today."

"How's that?"

"Turned out it was cancer, and Doc Somerville cut my balls off. I ain't a man no more but at least I'm alive."

"Jesus, that's awful."

"That's what everyone thinks, but it ain't so bad. I put on about thirty pounds, is all." That probably meant he had been about 250 to start with.

"What about, well . . ."

"That's the part that ain't as bad as folks think. You just don't care no more. Some pretty little old gal could walk down the road there bare-ass naked and I wouldn't think no more about it than if she was a tree or something."

"You must remember what it was like, though."

"Well, that's the thing people don't understand. I remember what it was like, all right, but I can't see what all the excitement was about no more. I remember doing it, but I can't see why I ever wanted to."

"And it doesn't bother you?"

"Hell, no. It's kind of peaceful. One more thing off your mind. I told my wife, I said, 'Sally May, I'll understand if you want to take up with somebody else,' and so she went off and done it. Another thing off my mind."

"So you went to work for Dr. Somerville?"

"Soon as I healed up. Stayed with him till he died."

"What kind of a boss was he?"

"I would have given you a different answer back then than what I might today."

"How about back then?"

"He was the nicest fellow you'd ever want to meet. You take most folks like that, doctors and all, most of them think their snot can make coleslaw. Dr. Denton wasn't like that. He was more like a regular person."

"How do you mean regular?"

The big man thought about what regular meant. "Well, you take your big-shot type of a person, if you happen to notice it, mostly they won't never actually touch the help," he said. "The doc, though, he'd go right ahead and sling his arm around me and talk into my ear the same way he would with the governor or some bank president.

"I don't mean to say he was buddy-buddy with me, exactly. He was the boss, and the both of us knew that. But he'd still treat a man like a human being. He'd ask me about things, and listen to what I said back. He'd tell me jokes or stories about when he was in school learning to be a doctor and stuff. He'd ask what did I think of this man or that man, folks he was doing business with and I'd know them from having them in the car.

"What it was like, now I come to think about it, it was almost like I was kin. Maybe like a nephew or a cousin that had some bad luck and he was helping me get back on my feet. Not close family like a son or a brother, but kin. It was us against them, you know what I mean?"

I didn't really know, since in my own family it had always been me against them. But I nodded as if I did.

"Of course, the Somervilles didn't have no real family," Harmon said. "Kids of their own, I mean."

"Why was that?"

"He had himself fixed so all he shot was blanks."

"Sometimes they can turn that around," I said. "Why didn't they hitch the plumbing back up once he got married?"

"Once he got married was when he had it done. Right after they come back from their honeymoon. They didn't neither of them want no kids."

"Why was that?"

"All they needed was each other, didn't want nobody else in between. One time I was driving him out to the airport to pick up the missus and I happened to mention something about kids. 'Well, you take a look at the president and Nancy sometime,' he says to me. 'You think they're glad they had kids? Should've found them a good abortionist out there in Hollywood, they'd've been a damned sight happier.' "

"I imagine they would have," I said.

"I wouldn't know," Harmon said. "Tell you the truth, it was the first I heard that Reagan even had any kids."

"They farmed them out mostly."

"Wanted to be alone, I reckon. The Somervilles was like that, too. One time I remember Doc Somerville says did I know any kids that was assholes, and I said sure I did. Well, he says, was their daddy and their mommy assholes, too? and I says sometimes maybe, but not necessarily. See, he says, me and the missus might just as easy have an asshole for a kid like those folks done."

Probably even easier, I thought, remembering Mendel and his sweet peas.

Harmon rubbed delicately with a little piece of steel wool at some blemish on his tin can and held it up to the light to check the surface. He said, "Last year I come across a magazine in the dump with the doc's picture on the front, so I carried it home and went to work on it. Far as I could make out from what they was saying, he knew right from the start them bonds he was selling wasn't worth nothing. You know if that's right?"

"Yes, that's right."

"What do you think of a man that would sell something like them bonds to a poor man?"

"Not much."

"You damn right not much. That's what he done to me, though, his own driver."

"I heard he did that."

"Well, you heard right. I must have carried millions of dollars for him and never a dime missing, and he gone and done me like that."

"Carried millions of dollars where?"

"Whenever he didn't need the car, I'd go around with a bag and put cash money in banks all over Houston."

"In whose name?"

"Different names, but mostly the missus."

"Who'd fill out the deposit slips?"

"They was always in her writing, no matter what the name was on them. The way it would work, every time I'd make a deposit I'd pick up a couple of them slips and put them in the bag for her to use next time."

"How much were the deposits for?"

"Somewheres between nine thousand and ten thousand."

"Ever actually ten thousand?"

"No, always a hundred dollars, two hundred dollars short." Harmon had been what the drug dealers call a smurf. A courier who spreads money all over town, in amounts just below ten thousand dollars. Transactions larger than that have to be reported to the IRS.

"Nobody ever asked you why you were depositing all this cash for somebody else?"

"Why would they care, long as they got the money?"

Harmon was right, of course. Banks take money from the Mafia, the Medellín cartel, political consultants, pimps, corporate raiders, Scientologists, TV preachers, any kind of human scum and no questions asked. The way a bank looks at money, it's all green.

"Was this money in savings accounts or checking?"

"Checking."

"How many deposits would you make, say in a week?"

"Oh, seven or eight a week anyway. Sometimes a lot more."

Millions a year in non-interest-bearing accounts, then. Which meant Somerville had passed up hundreds of thousands of dollars in interest.

"How long did this go on?"

"Well, what I'm talking about here, doing it every day, that wasn't for but a year or two before he died."

When everything was starting to unravel, that is, and indictments were starting to come down. Somerville must have been skimming as hard as he could, while he was still able to get his hands into the cash flow. Spread around in relatively small accounts, it would probably be out of the reach of debtors or the government.

"Did you ever wonder about what you were doing?" I asked.

"Whatever Doc Somerville wanted was all right with me. He saved my life and then doe gave me the best job I ever had. Far as I was concerned, the sun rose and set in that man."

"How did you feel about Mrs. Somerville?"

"We got along real good. She knew I lived for the boss, just the same as she did."

"What did she look like?" I had seen pictures of her in the newspaper files, but microfilm doesn't give you any more than a rough idea. She had seemed decorative and small and trim.

"Fine-looking blond woman," Harmon Harmon said. "Reminded me a little bit of Dolly Parton, only not such big tits and dressed different. Mostly she'd wear dark blue or dark gray dresses. She wore a pearl necklace and little pearl earrings. Big pearl in the engagement ring he give her. Pearls was the onliest kind of jewelry she'd wear."

Somerville had been a quiet dresser, too, judging by a color photo that *Life* magazine ran of him. His silk tie was a muted paisley. His shirt had buttoned-down collars, which must have been unusual in Houston. He wore a natural-shouldered, narrow-lapeled suit a lot like the two I bought used from Keezer's in Cambridge years ago, only his probably cost $1,800 a copy instead of $40. And mine were dark blue and charcoal gray, power colors for the powerless. Somerville's was brown, the friendly color that salesmen wear. Reagan wore brown a lot.

In the picture, Dr. Denton had a high forehead, the kind of pattern baldness that probably started in his twenties and then changed its mind and didn't go any higher. His brown hair lay flat on the top of his head and was combed over his ears on the sides in his only stab at modishness. He wasn't handsome and he wasn't ugly, just another grown-up-kid American face. Although he was soft-looking rather than fat, the plump cheeks showed that he had to watch his weight. I couldn't tell his height from the picture.

"How tall a man was Somerville?" I asked.

"Average," Harmon said. "About like you." Average to a man Harmon's size, anyway. I was five eleven. Or just short of six feet, as Dr. Denton most likely tended to think of it, too. We probably both went about 180, but mine was a lot more serviceable, to judge by those cheeks and jowls in the photo.

"She looks small in her pictures."

"Oh, yeah, she wasn't but a little bit of a thing. Pretty little blond lady."

"Must have been hard on her after he died, if they were close like you say."

"I couldn't tell you. She let me go right after the funeral. Said having me around reminded her of him and she couldn't bear it. Same reason she give for closing the house down and letting all the rest of the staff go, too. I was sorry to leave, but I could understand how she felt. She gave me a month's pay and a real nice letter, too, not that I figured I'd need either one. I didn't know at the time that every penny of my so-called retirement fund had already went down the toilet. One way of looking at it, you could say I was putting my own life's savings into those bank accounts of Miz Somerville's."

"What do you suppose she's done with all that money?"

"Be damned if I know. Maybe took it off on her boat with her."

"She got a safe on the boat?"

"I couldn't tell you. I was never downstairs."

"You didn't go out with them?"

"No, mostly they'd go out alone. They loved going on that boat. That was their main hobby, driving that boat around. That and theirselves. I guess you could say that their real main hobby was each other."

"Didn't they ever have any fights?"

"Not so's you could say really. If she wanted something, he'd give it to her. And whatever he wanted, she'd give it to him, too. Mostly what he'd want was for her to tell him all the time how much she loved him and how wonderful he was, and how smart and good-looking and all.

"And I would have told you the same exact thing, to tell you the truth, until I got hold of that magazine and figured out that the son of a bitch had robbed me blind. Now I hope he rots in hell. I didn't even know what a bond was, till one day he told me I ought to take all my money out of Sunbanc and buy these new bonds with it. Told me right to my face I couldn't lose, made me a cement promise, and he was lying. Magazine said he knew it all the time, that those things was worthless as tits on a nun."

"He knew, all right," I said. "In the court documents there's a memo from him to his bond salesmen. He gave them orders to go after the weak and the meek and the ignorant, those were the exact words in the memo, and never tell them those bonds weren't backed by the government."

"The ignorant," Harmon Harmon said. "You looking right at him. So here I am living out of a dump. Ten years too young for the Social Security, ten years too old to find a job, not a goddamned nickel to my name and no balls to boot. Well, it ain't right to blame no balls on Doc Somerville, but the rest of it I got to fault him for."

"You have any idea where she goes with her boat?" I asked.

"I can't tell you for sure, no. But I can tell you what they was always talking about doing when they got old. Their idea was to spend Christmas here in Houston, then head on down to the Bahamas for a while. Then follow the warm weather along the coast up to Canada, then back down in the fall and do her all over again."

"They ever talk about a place in Maine called Islesboro?"

"Oh, yeah. A couple of other Houston big shots spend the summers up there, and they'd talk about when they visited them."

"What other places did they talk about?"

"Fishers Island. Charleston. Someplace in Florida, some island. Annabelle Island?"

"Sanibel?"

"Something like that. I only remember the places I heard of before. I wouldn't have remembered that place in Maine if you hadn't said the name."

I sat and talked with Harmon H. Harmon for another hour. Once you got used to the smell, he was good company. But talking to him didn't get me any closer to the money Somerville had stolen from my old men. Plenty of business had been discussed in the back of the limousine by Somerville and his associates, but Harmon hadn't been able to follow most of the discussion. "They was always talking about fucking this one and fucking that one," Harmon said, "but when they started in about how they was going to do the actual fucking, I most generally couldn't follow what they was talking about. It all sounded like them guys at the carnival to me, moving them cups around so fast that a man don't have any idea where the pea is at."

Finally I got up to go and he got up to see me out, the whole bus shifting with the weight of him. Outside I said, "Harmon, you mind if I ask you something personal?"

"Go right ahead."

"Well, where do you get food and water?"

"I fill jugs from a house about a half-mile down, around that bend there. Food I get Saturdays. After he pays me for the day, the fella runs the dump lets me take his pickup to the grocery. Them fellas own the grocery, they let me pick through the spoiled fruits and vegetables back of the produce section. Then maybe I'll buy me some baloney and Vienna sausages, and some canned stuff, and a bunch of bread and doughnuts. Maybe some cookies and candy, soda pop. All depending on how I feel."

"That's enough, huh?"

"Oh, hell, yes. You'd be amazed how much they throw away in a store. Least little thing wrong with something, won't nobody buy it. But that don't mean it ain't good."

"I guess it doesn't," I said. "My other question is where do you shit?"

Harmon pointed to an entrenching tool leaning against the bus. "Same place a bear does," he said. "I just scratch me a little hole in the woods and hunker down."

"You pretty much got it whipped, Harmon," I said,

and meant it. "Plenty of people with money live a lot worse than you do."

I didn't mean physically, and Harmon understood that. "Well, it ain't the Ritz," he said. "But if a man's got the Ritz they can take it away from him. The bastards can't take away what I got. You know what I mean?"

"Sort of, but go ahead."

"What I mean is this bus ain't mine anyway. It was just setting here empty. The bastards could even blow the fucking thing up and everything in it and still I wouldn't have lost nothing. You know why not?"

"Why not?"

" 'Cause everything inside that bus come from in here where the fuckers can't get at it." He tapped his head. "I'd just make it all again, only better. So all them Dr. Somervilles, I got their number."

8

THE NEWS WAS BAD IN Washington, as usual. But this time the bad news was personal, not public.

I was in a cheap motel in South Carolina run by some people named Patel. Call anybody Patel who is sitting at the desk of a cheap motel in the south, and you'll be right two times out of three. The first Patel to arrive here from the Indian subcontinent must have liked what he found, and sent back for six or eight thousand relatives.

Being new arrivals, and honest by American hotel standards, the Patels have not yet begun to add a surcharge to your bill for making credit card calls that don't cost management a dime. Mine was to Hope Edwards. Her husband, Martin, answered, and we acted pleasant and civilized. Maybe he wasn't acting. It was quite possible he knew his wife and I had been lovers for years, and didn't care, or was even glad for her sake. I was acting, though. I never felt pleasant or civilized talking to Martin. I felt guilty, and jealous, and resentful, and superior, and inferior, and all sorts of other things—none of them particularly creditable, or intelligent.

"Great to hear from you," Martin said. "Hope said she had a wonderful lunch with you the other week. Wish you'd had a chance to drop by while you were in town. Hold on, I'll get her."

Well, we'd had two wonderful lunches, actually. But one lunch would have sounded like no big thing to her husband, and two lunches would have been pushing it. Love makes liars of us all.

Over time you get used to it, of course, and we had had plenty of time. When we met, back in 1980, she was on leave from the White House to work in the Carter campaign. I had just jumped over to the Carter camp myself, since Teddy had missed getting the nomination. A lot of people had jumped over, which is okay and normal in politics. The victorious captain picks up crewmen from the ships he's sunk. There was no obvious spot for me, since a sitting president is already overstocked with pilots, gofers, and name rememberers. But a couple of my Kennedy acquaintances sold me to the Carter people as a security expert, on the grounds that I had worked with the CIA in Laos. Strictly speaking this was true, since I spent a few very profitable years with Air America, the CIA's little air force in Southeast Asia. Actually though it was blue smoke, since all I did was fly planes for them. But that's politics for you, blue smoke. And I was able to fake my way, since nobody else in the campaign knew much about internal security, either. Not that they didn't need it, with William Casey handling dirty tricks for the other side. In fact they needed a lot more than I was able to provide, as it turned out.

Anyway, Hope and I met on the road during the general campaign, on the plane. The plane and headquarters are the two centers of power in a campaign, with the plane more powerful because that's where the candidate usually is. Most of the time on the plane you're not on the plane, of course, you're on buses and in hotels and at hog farms and Legion Halls and fairgrounds and all the other places you go to get your picture and a few words on the evening news, which is the whole point of the otherwise idiotic exercise.

And so we started our lovers' lies on the plane, as it were, back in the autumn of 1980. It didn't matter for me, with a divorced wife back in Alaska, but it mattered for Hope. Everybody on the plane knew she was married, and many of them even knew her husband and kids back in Washington. And so while practically everybody else on the plane was bouncing from bedroom to bedroom carefree as rabbits, we were setting our alarms for absurdly early hours so we could sneak back to wherever we belonged before the wake-up guy came around and the corridors filled with people.

In a way it was kind of fun, adding a little interest to things. And in lots of other ways it was kind of sad. Right now was one of the sad parts. I wished Hope were free to be here, to laugh with me at Mr. Patel's room. But she was up there in Washington, where I heard her steps approaching the phone.

"Hey," she said.

"Hey yourself. I'm in a motel in South Carolina and if I had a couple of quarters I could make the bed vibrate for ten minutes. It's a feature here. They call it Magic Fingers."

"Oh, Tom, I'm terribly happy for you. I truly am."

"They've got X-rated TV, too. Speaking of which, how about a long lunch at the Tabard Wednesday?"

"Damn, I can't. A special all-day board meeting came up, and I won't be able to get away for lunch."

"I can stay over. How about Thursday? Friday?"

"Thursday morning I fly to Aspen for a three-day conference."

"Shit."

"You're absolutely right. Look, I'll duck out at lunchtime anyhow and the hell with them. The way the meetings are scheduled, though, it'll have to be a fast one. Twelve-thirty? Call me first thing Wednesday morning at the office, though, in case I have to cancel at the last minute."

I got into Washington late Tuesday night, and called her next morning. She didn't have to cancel. But it wound up being one of those lunches confined strictly to the dining room, which isn't my favorite kind of lunch with Hope but is a lot better than nothing at all. I had the house salad and a pot of tea, so that I could tell her about the Houston trip while she stoked up for the afternoon's meeting with her board of directors.

"Was he badly hurt?" she asked after I had told her about Hostetter, leaving out the gun.

"I guess it couldn't have been that bad," I said. "There was nothing about him in the papers the next day, or on the radio." I figured this probably meant he was alive, since his connection with the Sunbanc Savings and Loan collapse would have made his death news. Alive, he probably wouldn't have complained to the police about tripping over a pipe while running away from a man he had just kidnapped at gunpoint. He would have passed the incident off as an accident.

"What do you think Hostetter was up to?" Hope asked.

"Probably just what he said. Dr. Potter probably figured I was a thief or a con man after Billene, and he sent Hostetter to scare me away."

"What if the thief or con man were Potter himself?"

"It's a possibility. But he still wouldn't want me horning in."

"No, I guess not."

"Although I don't know how I could horn in. He's the executor. For all we know, he's already robbed her blind and there's nothing left. Probably he could even do it legally, couldn't he?"

"It's been done, all right, although it's easier to get away with if you're a lawyer. There's a lot of room for judgment calls in managing an estate, and poor judgment isn't a crime. At least up to a point."

"I think I'm reaching that point myself," I said. "It'll be a crime if I spend any more of the old guys' money. All I know for sure is that at one point Somerville was parking millions of dollars in small accounts all over Houston. I don't know where it is now, and if I knew I couldn't get it back. Certainly not legally. When you get into the world of wire transfers, foreign bank accounts, dummy corporations, hidden assets, holding companies, well, shit, you're helpless. Far as I can tell, the law is on the side of the thieves."

"I hate to say it," Hope said, "but you're right. So what do you do?"

"I go back to Cambridge, charge the old men a few bucks for expenses so they won't feel like charity cases, and forget about the whole thing."

"That's what you should do, all right, but of course you won't forget it."

"Eventually I will."

"Sure, like you forgot it when Carter boycotted the Olympics."

The reason I had gone to work in Iowa for Teddy

Kennedy was to help him beat Carter in the primaries. When Kennedy flamed out, I was still mad about the boycott. But by then I was hooked on the weirdness of campaigning. And once Carter got the nomination, his game became the only one in town for a Democrat.

Hope reached across the table and touched my hand lightly. "At least I got to see you," she said. "I'm sorry about this business with my board."

I was sorry, too, and at the same time not sorry. Later I thought about it up in my room, where I had gone for a little brooding and self-pity after Hope had gone off about her business.

I was wishing she were with me, yet in a curious way I was also relieved that her job came second. And her family came first. And I only came third. Why? Why wouldn't I want her undivided attention? Wasn't that supposed to be how love worked? But supposed and is are different. If Hope weren't reliable and responsible toward her family and her job, she'd be another person. I don't think I'd love that other person quite as much as I do this one.

But I still wished she had called in sick. The hell with it, I thought. I'll show her. I'll hold my breath until I die, and then she'll be sorry. Or if actual death seems a little too permanent, I'll subject myself to the next worst thing.

It was one o'clock in the afternoon, and in only nine hours of straight driving on the interstates I could be safe at home in Cambridge. Also, it looked like it was about to rain. Perfect. I got my bags out of the closet.

It rained all the way up, making for an eleven-hour trip. And it rained the next day, and the day after that, and it was raining this morning, too. I was sitting in The Tasty watching the raindrops slide down the window.

Joey Neary collected from a customer, rang it up, and came over to where I was sitting in front of a half-full cup of lukewarm tea, made from the kind of teabag that comes in big institutional boxes and says nothing on the tag except ORANGE PEKOE. There was one other customer in the place, an Ethiopian cab driver too far away to hear and too new off the boat to understand anyway.

"I'm sorry about last night, man," Joey said. "I really am."

"It's okay."

"No, I got you into it. You went down there as a favor to me."

"No, I didn't, Joey. I did it because I figured it wasn't raining in Houston. Which it wasn't."

"Hey, don't shit a shitter, okay. I feel bad."

"Joey, it's natural the old guys were disappointed."

"It's not natural they act like that. That fucking Mooney, they should have sat on his head. I was ashamed for them."

"Their hopes were up. They had to take it out on somebody."

What I didn't want Joey to know, what I was glad to see he hadn't picked up on, was that I had done my best to make sure the Dummy Dozen took it out on me. The meeting with them had been last night, at the home of the oldest member, Marty Maginnis. Maginnis's little house was way out Garden Street near St. Peter's Field, and by the looks of the furniture he had lived there since the wedding gifts came in, more than a half century ago. There was a Mrs. Maginnis, who met us and went upstairs to leave the menfolk to their business. She had set up a card table covered with a paper tablecloth. On it were big plastic bottles of soft drinks, paper cups, and paper plates for the cookies. They were the kind of supermarket cookies you fish out of clear plastic bins with clear plastic tongs and pay for by the pound. We helped ourselves, and the lucky ones found places on the couch, the armchair, or the four straight chairs dragged in from the dining room. The rest of us stood. I stood, although Maginnis had offered me a chair. I wanted to talk down to them.

When I was finished telling them what little I had learned in Houston, Joey's uncle Kevin said, "What about this P.J. Potter? What sort of a man is he?"

"Very friendly," I said. "Full of smiles."

"Did you tell him what happened to us?"

"I didn't bother."

"It sounds like he might be the kind of man who'd listen."

"He's not, take my word for it. You feel sorry for a lamb chop? That's how sorry he'd feel for guys like you. You're what he eats. People that are weak, meek, and ignorant."

"Maybe he doesn't know what happened below him in the organization," said Ed Cleary. He was the man who had cashed in his pension rights for money to buy Somerville's worthless bonds.

"That's what the serfs kept saying in Russia," I said. "Every time the czar's men would give them another kick in the balls, the poor dumb serfs would tell one another, 'This shit would never happen if only the czar knew.' Believe me, the czar knew. Believe me, Potter knew. The fact is, he doesn't care what happens to you serfs. You're his meat."

"We're not serfs," the old man named Chris Costello said. In a room full of Irishmen, somebody had to get hot sooner or later.

"To a guy like Potter you are. Every two years you prove it when you go out and vote for guys that are going to fuck you."

"Harry here, maybe," Cleary said, pointing to an old-timer who hadn't been at the earlier meetings. "He voted for Reagan and then for this new one, too. But I never voted for a Republican in my life."

"No difference between Republicans and Democrats," I said. "Look at Tip O'Neill. You voted for Tip, didn't you?"

"Of course."

Speaker O'Neill had represented the Eighth Congressional District since Jack Kennedy left the seat open in 1952 to run for the Senate. When he retired in 1986, he returned the seat to the Kennedys—Joe Kennedy, Jr. It was a lock that nobody in the room had ever voted against Tip.

"Well, Tip put Jim Wright in as Speaker when he retired," I said. "And Wright was an errand boy for Somerville and the rest of them."

"Tip never took a nickel in his life," said Marty Maginnis. Now things were heating up a little.

"I never said he did. I just said all those guys in Washington play the game, and guys like Somerville and Potter run the game."

"Tip didn't play the game."

"Hey, okay. Not Tip. I'm just making a general point, here, all right? That guys like Potter treat guys like you like serfs. They don't say they're sorry and give you your money back, is all I'm saying."

"How about the courts?"

"What do you think?" I asked.

They thought this over a minute, and then the stumpy old guy named Brian Mooney came up with the right answer: "They run the courts, them guys," he said.

"Yeah, that's all the law is," one of the old men said. "Money talks, bullshit walks."

"What can we do, then?" Marty Maginnis asked.

"Legally, nothing that won't cost more than you'd get back. Illegally, there's probably nothing, too. Maybe in the movies it's okay to steal from the rich and give it to the poor. Only when you do it in real life you go to jail."

"Nobody's asking you to do anything like that."

"I hope not, Mr. Maginnis. I don't break the law."

"Nobody said you did."

"The fact is the law says buyer beware. You guys weren't exactly beware, were you?"

"If you're saying we were a bunch of damned fools, we're aware of that."

"I told you going in, that there was probably nothing I could do for you. Didn't I?"

"You did," said Maginnis. "We were just hoping. Betting on a long shot, you might say."

"Damned long," Mr. Mooney said. He was a red-faced little man, and he seemed meaner than the others.

"What do you mean by that?" I said.

"I mean you're nothing but some guy that Kevin's nephew says hello to at work. I told you, Marty. Didn't I tell you we should have hired a lawyer?"

"Try hiring a lawyer for seven hundred and change in expenses," I said.

"You said it would be four or five hundred," Mooney said. He *was* kind of a mean little shit, even if I had provoked him on purpose.

"Tell you what," I said, "I'll give you the receipts."

"Brian, for Christ's sake," Maginnis said. "The man spent a couple weeks on it and didn't charge us a dime except expenses. Don't listen to him, Tom. Of course we'll pay you back."

"Don't if you don't want to," I said. "This guy thinks it's high, fuck it. I'd rather eat the seven hundred than argue."

"We'll pay every dime. You can count on that."

"Look, I'm sorry I disappointed you guys and I hope you get your three hundred thousand back somehow, but I couldn't do it, and I don't think anybody else can either, and I told you that up front. It makes you feel good, give me a few bucks for gas money. Or don't. I met some nice people, got a little sun. The hell with the whole thing."

A couple of them tried to smooth things over, but I left while there was still bad feeling. I didn't want them just to be disappointed. I wanted their memory of me to be vaguely unpleasant, something they'd gratefully put behind them and forget.

Now Joey Neary took my teapot over to the machine and refilled it with hot water. He left the same tea bag in it, but even free hot water was a first for Joey, who watched the owner's nickels as if they were his own.

"Here, man," Joey said, pulling an envelope out of his hip pocket. "It's only four hundred dollars, but they'll have the rest next week."

"I told them, Joey. I don't really want it."

"Take it, all right? You want to make everybody feel like a shit?"

"But it's okay for me to feel like a shit, huh?"

"Will you just fucking take it? Jesus, you spent it, didn't you? I was trying to tell that fucking Mooney after you left, him and Costello, they should try it themselves, driving down to Houston and back on seven hundred bucks."

I took the money.

"What got some of them going," Joey said, "it was when you dumped on Tip. Those guys, Tip can do no wrong."

"I shouldn't have said that. But it's true he backed Wright, and it's true Wright carried a lot of water for guys like Dr. Denton."

"Yeah, but—"

"Yeah, but I still shouldn't have said it. I know. I'm sorry."

"Tip didn't steal, you know. That's why he had to make money doing them TV ads, because he didn't steal when he could have."

"I know that. That's why I'm sorry."

"Well, fuck, I'm sorry, too. Sorry I ever got you into the whole goddamned thing."

"Hey, we're both sorry, and it's over, and I got seconds on my tea, which I never heard of before, so let's put it behind us. Really."

"I still—"

"Joey, will you shut the fuck up? It never happened. It's over."

That night I used a little bit of the four hundred dollars, which was all in fives, tens, and twenties, to take Felicia Lamport out to dinner. Her husband knew Felicia and I went out together, and so did Hope. It had been going on for years, ever since I sneaked into a course of Felicia's at the Harvard extension school and she caught me.

Tonight, as always, we went to the Thai place near my apartment, where the waiters all knew Felicia and would tell the cooks to chop up a couple extra hot peppers for her. While she ate, the cooks would come to the kitchen door and sneak peeks at the round-eye with the asbestos mouth. "At my age," she told me once, "the taste buds are somewhere between languid and dead. It requires considerable insistence to get their attention." I never knew exactly what her age was, but I knew from the papers that her husband, a semiretired Episcopalian bishop, was in his late seventies. He was in the papers because he kept getting arrested in antiwar demonstrations. The bishop thought the police had it wrong way around. The bishop's position was that the cops should be arresting everybody who wore a yellow ribbon.

"Have you ever heard of a guy named Albert Jay Nock?" I asked Felicia while we were waiting for the food.

"*Memoirs of a Superfluous Man?*" she said. "Of course I have. Why do you think I let you take my class for nothing, instead of throwing you out as you no doubt richly deserved?"

"Well, why?"

"Because I recognized immediately that you belonged to the Remnant."

Nock's theory is that most people fail to act like human beings because they in fact aren't human beings but a subhuman species he calls mass-man. Now and then a human being is born to a mass-man and a mass-woman, for reasons no one knows. These very few human beings are what Nock calls the Remnant.

"I'm flattered," I said.

"As well you might be. Now tell me instantly why you want the keys to our place in Islesboro. It seems a little odd, frankly, since I've been inviting you up for years and you've never come."

And so I told her exactly why, which I hadn't done with Hope. Hope is not a criminal at heart. Felicia, being a poet, is. So, in his way, is the bishop. But what I had in mind wasn't quite the bishop's way, and I knew she'd never mention my plan to him any more than I'd tell Hope.

"I may wind up not needing the keys," I said at the end. "It sounds like the kind of place where strangers draw too much attention. But I don't know what I'll find. I might miss the last ferry back to the mainland, or some damned thing, and have to spend a night or two on the island."

"Well, you could park in the barn and lock yourself in the house if you needed to," she said. "Nobody would know there was anybody inside as long as you kept away from the windows on the side facing the road and didn't use the lights."

Felicia was having no trouble at all putting herself in a criminal frame of mind; basically, she was a slight, white-haired, little old lady outlaw.

"You want to go up in May, you say? The plumber may not have come by to turn the water on by then. We never go up before July. I could call him, I suppose, but it might not be a good idea to have any deviation from routine. What do you think?"

"It doesn't really matter whether the water's turned on. Even if the Billene is up there . . ."

"They call this woman the Billene, do they? Like the Donald? That's wonderful."

"It's the name of the boat."

"Oh, I'm so disappointed. Go on, though."

"Even if the Billene turns out to be up there, I'll be staying on the mainland. There's a campground near Lincolnville where I can be anonymous. The whole thing depends on nobody knowing who I am. All I'd be likely to need your house for is to make phone calls or to stay out of sight for a few hours. Get away from the blackflies."

"They won't be too bad till later on. Well, of course you can have the keys, Tom. Are you sure I wouldn't be any help? I could tell the bishop I was going up for a few days to put some early things in the garden. Actually I did that one May. The deer ate every plant. They're so pretty and graceful. If you see any of them around the place, you will shoot them, won't you?"

9

TAKE OVER YOUR HUSBAND'S
seat in the House of Representatives in 1940, move on
to the U.S. Senate eight years later, spend another twenty-four years there, lose your seat, then die. And in
Maine they will name a ferryboat after you. It will shut-
tle back and forth between Lincolnville and Islesboro
until long after you yourself are forgotten by practically
everybody but politics groupies with weird trick memories. Like me. I remembered that Margaret Chase Smith
had cast the key vote for Nixon's dumb and insane Anti-
ballistic Missile Treaty in 1969. *Margaret Chase Smith*
was giving the public much more useful service now.

The line to board had been long; nobody was likely
to notice an old Datsun with Massachusetts plates.
Most of the people stayed in their cars for the twenty-
minute crossing, so I did, too. The sea was a dull gray,
the color of engine dirt. The sky was patchy, with the
sun breaking through the overcast off and on, as it

had been doing all through the two-hundred-odd miles from Cambridge.

Islesboro was low and covered with hemlock and spruce woods, like all the other islands in sight, and like the mainland, too. Just outside the small port a sign said ISLESBORO—DEDICATED TO EDUCATIONAL EXCELLENCE. I figured this meant the local politicians were too mean to spend money on the schools, when signs were so much cheaper. I'd figure the exact same thing about a man who told everybody he wanted to be the "education president."

Following Felicia's directions, I made a circuit of the island. It was a pleasant, pretty place with a couple of general stores, a post office, a volunteer fire department, and a miniature library open three afternoons a week. All this was spread out over miles of country. The closest thing to a center was Dark Harbor, down at the south end of the long, skinny island, and its two or three shops were closed for the season. It was only the first week in May.

The major activity on Islesboro at the moment was getting ready for the summer people. Painters were up on ladders. A couple of linemen were getting tools out of an orange and white electric company truck. I saw a plumber's truck parked in a driveway, probably the same man who turned on Felicia's system every spring. Islesboro didn't look big enough to support more than one plumber.

I headed north from Dark Harbor toward the house where the bishop and Felicia spent their summers. To reach it you turned right at Durkee's General Store and down a road that dead-ended into the water. Just before the end you went right a few hundred yards on a dirt road, and there it was up on a hill to the right: a good-sized Victorian painted blue with white trim. A log lay across the driveway to keep people out, but it wasn't a very big log. I stopped and looked around to make sure no one was in sight, and then bumped the car right over it and went up the long driveway. I parked behind the house. As Felicia had said, this put me out of sight from the road. If I needed to get the car completely out of sight, I had the key to the padlock on the small barn behind the house.

I also had the key to the kitchen door, and I got the disused lock to work after a little fiddling. I went through the rooms quickly. The dining room and living room faced east toward the road and the sea beyond it. Both rooms were darkened by sheets of plywood nailed over the large windows. The weather probably came from that side, because the other ground-floor windows were unprotected. Upstairs were four bedrooms. The stripped beds were covered with newspaper to keep the sunlight from fading the mattresses. The rugs were folded double on the floor, with mothballs inside, as I found out when I crunched one underfoot. Books were everywhere, piled high on every dresser, stacked on the floor, crammed into plastic milk crates and flea market bookcases. Books I wanted to read, too. The first thing I spotted was one on a guy called the *pétomane*, a turn-of-the-century Frenchman who could suck both air and water up his rectum at will. I learned this from the dust jacket. Naturally I glanced inside. Evidently the *pétomane* worked on his gift until he was able to make a fortune in the music halls by farting tunes and blowing out candles from a distance. Well, maybe Felicia would mail me the book later. For now, I didn't want to hang around until somebody spotted me. I put the book back where I found it, and left.

Still following Felicia's directions, and the map of the island she had given me, I drove from her house to Captain Bob Patchen's boatyard. It was on the sheltered side of the island, farther on out toward the northern end. I found Captain Patchen past the boatyard itself, a quarter-mile farther down the road at his launching ramp.

He waved for me to come on over when I got out of my car. He was working the controls of a truck transmission sunk in a pit lined with cinder blocks. The transmission was powered by an electric motor. A cable ran from a winch into an underground tunnel that led to what looked like a section of railroad track coming up out of the ocean. As the cable paid out, the heavy sled on the other end of it was sliding down the rails into the sea. A large sailboat was held upright on the sled by an arrangement of booms and ropes that didn't look strong enough to keep it balanced. But a couple of men were standing alongside it, and they didn't look worried about it falling over on them.

"Captain Patchen?" I said, over the motor noise.

"That's me," he hollered back. "Be with you as soon as we get this thing in the water."

I sat down on a stump to watch as the ocean very gradually took up the weight of the boat and the two men climbed on board to cast off the lines holding it. Patchen manipulated his levers until the winch started to reel the cable in and the empty sled came slowly up out of the water on its rails. The two men had the boat under power, meanwhile, and were maneuvering it away from shore.

"What can I do for you?" Patchen said once he had cut the motor. He wore clean khaki pants, a polo shirt, and sneakers with no socks. Dressed like that, either he was a summer person who liked the life and went into business year-round, or he was an islander who grew up around the summer people. Probably the former, to judge from his generic East Coast accent. I told him how interested the *Globe* was in the life-styles of the formerly rich and famous.

"I always sort of liked the Somervilles, to tell you the truth," Captain Patchen said. "I thought he was just a doctor, till all the stories came out later on. He knew his way around a boat pretty well, and she was kind of a pleasant, cheerful little thing. Pretty woman. Very devoted to each other."

"Did they come up every summer?"

"Well, I'd have to check my books on that. Most summers they'd bring their boat by for us to haul it and go over the hull, but I don't think it was like clockwork. Seems to me they missed a year now and then."

"Would they stay long?"

"Just a week or ten days back when the doctor was alive."

"Long trip for just a few days."

"Oh, they wouldn't make the trip. They'd hire somebody to bring her up and back. They'd charter a plane for themselves."

"What would be the point? Why not just fly on up and stay in one of the inns?"

"There's no point to a lot of things some of these rich people do, except maybe to show off to one another. The Somervilles used the boat, though. They'd go on day trips, sometimes entertain their friends aboard. In those days they'd tie up in Dark Harbor, where a couple of other Texas people have houses. I don't think she sees people much now. They tie up in Sabbathday Harbor and go over to Camden for groceries."

"They being Mrs. Somerville and her crew?"

"Crew of one, yes. He must be a good sailor, because the boat's in good shape. But he looks more like a movie bad guy, not that he can help what he looks like."

"What kind of a guy is he really?"

"Hard to say. He doesn't talk much. If anybody'd know, Rodney Thornburgh would."

"Who's Rodney Thornburgh?"

"Rodney's a diver when he can get work."

"Is the diving business slow?"

"For him it is. A lot of people won't hire him because he's a lobster poacher."

"Supposed to be a hanging offense in Maine, isn't it?"

"Some people think it should be, but all Rodney got was two years in the state penitentiary down in Thomaston. Second time for him."

"What did he do the first time?"

"Broke into summer places, him and his cousin Earl. But Earl got off, as usual. They stored the stuff in Earl's barn, but Earl said he didn't know it was there, and Rodney backed him up."

"And this lobster poacher knows Mrs. Somerville's sailor or bodyguard, or whatever he is? What's the connection?"

"Mrs. Somerville hired him last year to clear a fouled propeller."

"She doesn't care that he poaches lobsters?"

"My guess is she doesn't know. She hardly ever leaves the boat except to shop and her man, Glen is his name, he doesn't talk much, like I said. Probably Glen hired Rodney out of the phone book. The fact is, Rodney's a damned good diver."

"How long does it take to clear a propeller?"

"It would depend. Oh, I see what you're driving at. No, you wouldn't be hanging around for days. But the propeller needed to be replaced, so Rodney had to order a new one shipped in, and then go out again to put it on. He had to be out there a couple times, probably for half a day or so. Probably Glen fed him coffee, let him use the head, that kind of stuff. I assume they probably talked about the job, what kind of shape the hull was in. I'm not saying they're buddies. Just that Rodney at least had some dealings with the man."

"Rodney's in the book, you say?"

"His name is in the Islesboro book as a diver, but it's his brother's number, really. His brother lives in the old Thornburgh house since the parents died. Rodney used to live there with him, but he pretty much wore out his welcome on the island. You could leave a message with his brother, only it might be a while before it gets through. Quickest way would be to drive up to Belfast and ask for him in Captain Billy's Saloon."

"Think he'd be there tonight?" It was a Monday, which used to be a slow night for business in my saloon days.

"Put it this way. I've never gone by Captain Billy's and not seen his car outside."

"I'll give it a try then. Let me ask you something else. Down in Houston they said the *Billene* follows the spring up here. Have any idea when she might arrive?"

"Last Friday, actually. She's anchored in Sabbathday Harbor same as last year."

"Where is Sabbathday Harbor?"

"Take a right when you hit the blacktop, then turn left at Durkee's Store. Road runs right down to Ryder's Cove and Sabbathday runs off to your right."

I wouldn't have any trouble finding it. It was the same bay Felicia's house was on, and I headed back there to see if I could spot the *Billene* from the upstairs windows.

This time I figured I might be in the house long enough to make it worthwhile getting the car completely out of sight. I ran it into the barn, padlocked the double doors, and let myself into the house again. Field glasses were in a downstairs closet, along with foul weather gear, fishing tackle, and a jumble of kids' games for the nieces and nephews. Felicia and the bishop had no children of their own but filled up the house with relatives over the summer.

I took the binoculars upstairs, where I could see over the trees that blocked the view of the ocean from downstairs. The *Billene* was hard to miss, a sixty-footer sitting way out in the bay, all shiny like a brand-new toy. The name on the bow came up well enough in the glasses so that I could just read it, although I might have had trouble if I hadn't known what word I was looking at. The distance was probably a quarter mile. I held the glasses on the boat for a few minutes but couldn't spot any movement through the curtained portholes. Somebody had to be aboard, though, since a little boat was sitting on top of the big boat. I'd say the little boat was on davits, except that I'm not entirely sure what davits are. I'd say it was a Whaler, too, except I'm not too solid on what Whalers are, either. But it was a hell of a big little boat. On Lake Champlain, where most of my nautical experience has been, you would have called it a big boat. It was blue and white like the yacht itself and had a big, black, powerful outboard attached to the rear end. Or stern, as we sailors call it.

After a while I put down the glasses. I went down and got the little book about the Frenchman who could play tunes out his ass. No reason I couldn't take in some biography while I kept an eye on the yacht. I had just got to the part where he was swimming in the Atlantic with some army buddies, still thinking his plumbing worked just like everybody else's, when suddenly a jet of icy water invaded his . . .

And suddenly I noticed a figure on the deck of the *Billene*. The figure could have been there for quite a while. That's how caught up I was in my story. The binoculars showed me a solidly built man wearing a sweat suit. With no one around for comparison purposes, it was hard to judge how tall he was. He was totally bald, without even the usual fringe of hair over the ears and round the back. His approach to coping with male pattern baldness was the same as Hostetter's back in Houston, only carried two steps further. First he was bald, and second he had a big mustache to show he could grow hair somewhere, at least.

Glen, the only name I had for him, began to do exercises on the deck. He started with twenty-five deep knee bends. Unimpressive. Then, warmed up, he did twenty more. Only this time they were one-legged ones, twenty on one leg and then twenty on the other. Impressive. Now thoroughly warmed up, he took his sweatshirt off. He had looked solid before, but with sweats it's hard to tell for sure. Now I could see that Glen was thick front to back, and side to side. He didn't have what body-builders call the Cobra, wide shoulders and lats tapering down to a wasp waist. Instead he had the kind of cylindrical build a lot of real weight lifters have, with a waist and hips as solid and nearly as big around as his chest.

After a series of breathing exercises, Glen went over to where the Whaler was and made a little hop up in the air toward it. Since he wound up hanging from its supports, there must have been handles or a bar up there, too small for me to make out from my distance. Whatever he had hold of, his hands were far apart, so that his arms and body made a Y. In slow motion he went up and down, up and down, fifty times. The best day I ever had I couldn't have matched that, not at his slow, muscle-grinding pace. Still hanging, he raised his legs, knees locked and toes pointed, up to chest level and down again. I didn't bother to count, but he did a lot of them. Then stretches. Odd to do them in the middle of a workout rather than at the beginning or the end, or both, but different strokes. Then an old calisthenics drill that I remembered from basic training: from standing to deep knee bend to push-up position, push-up with clapping hands at the top, back down, back to crouch, jump up in the air with hands over head, and repeat. I felt less inferior during this part of his session. He did a lot of repetitions, but his quickness and balance were nothing special. After a breather he wound up with twenty minutes skipping rope. No fancy rope-a-dope stuff. Just round and round, hop, hop, hop, till the mind numbs and the heart adapts to long, steady work.

At the end he barely stopped for breath before taking his shoes and sweatpants off. Underneath he wore a red Speedo, very snappy. Without a pause he went to the rail and dove into the water. I winced for him. In May, the ocean off Maine is cold enough to turn stones to prunes on contact. When he surfaced, he splashed strongly but not smoothly to the swim platform at the stern. Despite the Speedo, he was no Mark Spitz. He pulled himself easily up onto the diving platform at the stern, grabbed a towel from the deck above him, and made vigorous efforts to rub his skin off. No doubt he was making noises like a distressed walrus, too, although I was much too far away to hear.

Glen whatever returned below decks, and I returned to my book. The pétomane, I was happy to learn, had had more sense than Mohammed Ali and Sugar Ray and a lot of the rest of us. The Frenchman retired at the top of his game and returned to his hometown, where he lived comfortably off his winnings and eventually died of old age, surrounded by children, grandchildren, and great-grandchildren. We should all be so lucky, but won't.

Since I had nothing better to do, I killed the rest of

the day in the upstairs bedroom with Felicia's books. Whenever I thought of it I took a look at the motor yacht lying offshore. Once Glen reappeared, this time in jeans and sneakers and a blue denim work shirt. He spent three-quarters of an hour or so doing various chores on deck and then disappeared below. Once Billene came up, examined the sea and sky for a few minutes, and then went below again. She seemed to have kept her figure, although the distance was too great to tell how her face was holding up. At quarter to four I left to catch the last ferry. It didn't leave till four-thirty, but Felicia had warned me that there sometimes wasn't room for everyone. Sure enough, a line of cars was already waiting. I made it on board with no trouble, but a couple of cars didn't.

Back on the mainland, I headed a few miles south on Route 1 to Camden. Some of the shops were about to close, but I poked around the town for a while anyway. It was touristy enough to make lots of people go all nostalgic over how much more attractive and genuine it probably was in the good old days. But the fact is that the little boutiques and cute restaurants and all the rest of it are the only things that save plenty of small New England towns from being ugly, semirural slums. Take a look at old photos of some of those towns sometime, and it's not picture postcard stuff at all. Nostalgia is generally the sign of a poor memory.

After supper I headed back up Route 1 to Lincolnville, where the ferry was, and a mile or so past it to the campground. This early in the year it was nearly deserted. The manager waved an arm toward the woods and told me to grab any site that looked good to me. There was still plenty of light to set up my tent, which took only a few minutes. Aluminum shock cords have made the process as quick and easy as making up a bed.

Which I didn't bother to do. I just stuffed a couple of waffle mattresses inside, tossed a couple of pillows and blankets on top, and that was it. The rest of my gear—propane lantern, stove, folding chair, cooler full of food and drink, down sleeping bag in case it got really cold, five-cell police flashlight, combination radio-tape deck with earphones, electric lantern for reading inside the tent—I left in the car. It's relatively safe to leave gear in your tent when other campers are nearby, but not so safe when the place is practically deserted.

It was possibly too early for the Thornburgh boys to be out drinking, so I got the folding chair back out of the car and read a little more of the memoirs of Mr. Nock, the superfluous man. Eventually I came to, "Burke touches this matter of patriotism with a searching phrase. 'For us to love our country,' he said, 'our country ought to be lovely.' " What came to mind was Congress, the Supreme Court, and George Bush on a cigarette boat.

It was getting a little too dark to read, and so I headed up the road to Belfast. Captain Billy's Saloon turned out to be down by the bay. Three TV sets, each tuned to a different channel. Bumper pool, jukebox, a bar down one side and booths down the other, backlit Schlitz ads with colors so faded that by now everything looked vaguely green. Somebody had put on Patsy Cline singing "Who Can I Count On?," so maybe there was other decent stuff in the jukebox as well. Everybody looked up with either indifference or hostility when a stranger walked in. The hostility made me feel right at home. I had grown up in joints like this back home in upstate New York, and I had flashed the same fuck-you look at strangers a hundred times myself. So I smiled back at the crowd. If they wanted a dork from the city, I'd be one.

"Hi," I said to the bartender. "Cool beer signs. I love those old signs."

The bartender didn't say anything. I didn't blame him.

"Well, I guess I'll have a brew. Got a Lite?"

He was just turning to get it, when I figured I was carrying the joke too far. I'd rather drink the brine out of his pickled egg jar than Miller Lite. At least brine has a flavor. "Let me change my mind on that," I said. They didn't have any decent beer, though, so I had to settle for the next best thing. When he brought my Bud I asked him if he knew a couple of fellows named Earl and Rodney Thornburgh.

"Ayuh," he said.

"They here tonight?"

"Ayuh," he said again.

I swept the room and saw two possibilities sitting in a booth. One of them was built like a manatee.

"That them?"

"Ayuh."

"Big one Rodney?"

"Ayuh."

We don't exactly say "ayuh" in Port Henry, but they say a variant of it on the other side of Lake Champlain, in Vermont. Ayuh doesn't mean you don't talk much, or you'd come right out and say something like "That's the Thornburgh boys over there" and go on about your business. All that ayuh stuff is really a way of stringing the conversation out as long as possible. The closer you get to the Arctic Circle, the longer the winters get and the more time you've got to kill.

"Okay if I carry my glass?"

"Ayuh," the bartender said.

So I carried it over to the booth, and said, "Hi! Are you the Thornburgh boys?"

"Who the fuck wants to know?" the manatee said.

"Tom Henderson," I said, wagging my tail. "I'm a reporter for the *Boston Globe*."

"Oh, yeah?" the big one said, interested. "Well, yeah, I'm Rodney Thornburgh."

"Shut up, Rodney," the other one said. He was a good deal shorter than Rodney, and a great deal thinner. "What you want with Rodney?"

"Well, I'm doing a story on the Somerville fortune."

"Fortune?"

"Well, you know. Supposedly it was a billion-dollar empire."

"We don't know nothing about that. Why don't you ask Mrs. Somerville?"

"Oh, I will. You bet I will. But the way I like to do it, I like to ask everybody else before I go talk to the person themselves."

"How come you want to talk to Rodney?"

"Yeah, how come?" Rodney had the beer belly build of a biker, and like a surprising number of them, he had a higher voice than you'd expect to hear out of a tub that size.

"I heard you did some work on the boat. I thought maybe you could describe what it's like inside. You know, life-style stuff."

"You gonna put my name in the paper?"

"You want me to?"

He glanced at Cousin Earl for guidance and must have got it. "You better not put my name in," Rodney said.

"Then I won't. Mind if I sit down? Hey, how about a round? What are you guys drinking? Want to get something to eat? The paper's buying. You're Rodney, right? And you're . . . ?"

"Earl. Thornburgh."

"Brothers, huh?"

"Cousins."

"You're a diver, too, Earl?"

"I know how."

"I'll bet you do. Like Dwight Gooden knows how to pitch, huh? I heard Rodney is a really terrific diver, too."

I got drunk once with a deputy assistant secretary of state or something like that who was out in Laos on an inspection tour, playing "Secret War" up in the CIA base at Long Cheng. When I asked him how you got that high in a big bureaucracy, he said, "Flattery's the key. Nobody can resist it, even if he knows exactly what you're up to. You just slather it right on."

It wasn't advice I've been able to follow much, but now and then I can master the gag reflex for a while. And the guy was right. It always works. A few more minutes and it worked on Earl Thornburgh, who sat by and listened without objection while I asked his cousin about the life-style of Billene Somerville.

"She don't live no better than a lot of them that comes up here," Rodney said. "But I guess there's only so good you can live. Whatever she wants, she's got it."

"Like what?"

"Well, you know. Fancy clothes. Fancy stuff to eat."

"Where does she do her shopping?"

"Camden."

"How does that work? She send him over on the ferry?"

"What the fuck she need the ferry for? She lives on a boat, don't she?"

"I thought maybe it would be a pain in the ass to move a big boat like that once it's parked."

"Parked? You don't park no boats. You tie them up. Park the boat. You hear that, Earl?"

"I'm hearing a lot. Lot of talking." Earl had been looking sort of unhappy, come to think of it.

"Hey, listen, I don't want to take up too much of you

guys' time," I said. "Time's money, like the man said. That's why we get an allowance for our stories."

"Fuck's that mean, 'allowance'?" Earl said.

"Well, the paper sells information, right? I mean, isn't that what you pay for when you buy the paper? So if the paper sells it, the paper's got to expect to pay something for it, am I right? I mean, only logical, right? So they give us a story allowance."

"How much?"

"Not much. I only got two hundred dollars on this one."

"See, fuckhead?" Earl said to Rodney. "You was going to tell him for nothing, wasn't you?"

Rodney had no answer. That was exactly what he had been going to do, all right.

"Two hundred, huh?" Earl said, sounding tough, nobody's fool.

"Well, I've already spent a hundred."

"Let's see the other hundred, then."

"I've got more people to talk to. How about fifty?"

"Seventy-five."

"Aw, come on, guys. Well, okay." I fished the money out and handed it over. Earl pocketed it with a grin. He had outsmarted me, dumb shit that I was. Earl was a regular Donald Trump.

"Jesus, Rodney," Earl said to his cousin, shaking his head. Poor Rodney, totally clueless. When will they ever learn, the Rodneys of this world?

"So you untie the boat and off you go to Camden, huh?" I asked Rodney. "How does that work when you get there? You just tie up wherever there's a space?"

"You can drop anchor offshore and take the dinghy in. What they mostly do is go into the marina, though. Do everything at once. Top off their water tanks. Charge the batteries. Fill up on fuel. Like that."

"While she's going for groceries?"

"Right."

"How would she do that? She have a cart or something?"

"Lots of them do, yeah. But Mrs. Somerville has a fellow from Herb's Taxis that meets her. Takes her around to the different stores."

"While Glen's back at the marina taking care of the boat things?"

"Right."

"Glen his first name or his last?"

"All I know is Glen."

"How does she pay for the groceries? Cash or check?"

"Cash."

"What if she's shopping for clothes or something? Credit card?"

"Cash. At the marina, too."

"She gives Glen money for all the boat expenses?"

"I guess she gives it to him. He wouldn't pay out of his own pocket, would he?"

"Pay you in cash?"

"Always cash."

"It just occurred to me, how does the cab know when to pick her up?"

"They call ahead from the boat."

"Can you phone from boats?"

"Well, it's radio really, yeah. You never seen no phone lines to a boat, did you? But it's a phone, too. Same idea as a cordless."

"I never thought of that." And I hadn't, either. I knew about phoning from cars and planes, but for some reason it surprised me that you could just pick up a phone at sea and dial out. "Can you have TV on a boat?" I asked.

Earl and Rodney couldn't believe this dumb shit. "What do you think, for Christ's sake?" Rodney said. "Of course you can have TV. Boat that size, it's probably got at least a nine-kilowatt generator, forty-amp battery charging system."

"So you could have a regular home entertainment center?"

"You kidding me? All the bigger boats got that. Plus, a sixty-footer like the *Billene*, you probably got central vacuum, air conditioning, stove and microwave, washer-dryer, refrigerator, wet bar, icemaker, trash compactor. I'm just talking about the stuff that comes standard now. You can plug in anything you want on top of that."

"Like a computer? She got a computer?"

"I don't know. I never been below."

"You did all your business with Glen on deck?"

"On deck, or in the salon."

"Is that where she paid you, in the salon?"

"He paid me, Glen."

"In the salon, though?"

"One day in the salon, the other day on deck."

"Is the salon what he uses for an office? Like, is that where he got your money from?"

"No, he went below to get it."

"How come you want to know that?" Earl asked. Flattery and the seventy-five bucks may have quieted him down for a while, but they hadn't totally anesthetized him.

"Just trying to get a picture. The more details you know, the better you can write about something."

"You going to write about some guy going downstairs for money to pay a fucking diver?"

"I doubt it, but the thing is you never know. The way I work, I grab hold of everything and sort out what I need later. You in Nam?"

"Yeah. Me but not Rodney. Too young, wasn't you, Rodney? Just a kid."

"Reason I asked, what I just said about sorting things

out later, it reminded me of what guys would say in Nam when I was a correspondent there. Grunts would have it on their helmet. 'Kill 'em all and let the Lord sort 'em out later.' Ever see that?"

And so Earl and I told war stories for a while, me hoping it would make him stop wondering why the *Globe* would give a shit where Billene kept her stash. Or how she paid her bills or whether she had a computer. No reason the *Globe* wouldn't care about her love life, though. It ran stories about Marla and Ivana all the time.

"How did they seem to get along?" I asked Rodney. "Mrs. Somerville and Glen?"

"Okay, I guess. How do you mean?"

"I don't know. What did he call her, for instance?"

"Mrs. Somerville."

"And she called him Glen?"

"Right."

"Which could be his first name or his last one. Either of them ever touch each other? Hand on the shoulder, pat on the hand, anything?"

"Not that I seen."

"See anything to make you think they could have been getting it on?"

"Not so's you could tell."

"But you got to think about that, don't you? Two people living alone on a boat like that?"

"Boat like that'll sleep eight or nine people."

"Still, it was me out there on the ocean month in, month out, I'd be thinking about it. What does she look like? Still okay?"

"Got a nice ass."

"Definitely fuckable?"

"I wouldn't mind fucking her," Rodney said.

"That don't mean nothing," Earl said. "You'd fuck a snake if somebody'd hold it still for you."

"I seen you fuck stuff I had to hold still."

"I seen you talk too much, too."

"How about another round?" I said. "How about some of those pickled eggs? The *Globe*'s buying. You know, I used to go to this bar back home, the guy pickled his own eggs for forty years, the health department came by one day and told him he couldn't do it anymore. Health hazard. Old guy in his eighties came in there all the time, he said to the inspector, shit, these pickled eggs are what kept me alive this long . . ."

"Fuck pickled eggs," Earl said. "Me and Rodney got to take a piss." This looked like it was news to Rodney, but he got up and went along with his cousin, anyway. Earl was smooth, all right. He was certainly the brains of this outfit. He'd go at least five IQ points above cousin Rodney, although neither of them was anywhere near triple digits. Right now they'd be arguing at the urinal over Earl's rape of some sad, chinless farm girl while Rodney held her for him. I was beginning to dislike Earl pretty seriously.

But I had to ask him a few more questions, no matter how suspicious he was getting. I got ready to pull out the flattery again. Actually, though, I didn't need it. Earl acted friendly when he and Rodney came back from the toilet. Friendly didn't come natural to Earl, but he struggled with it.

"Got enough for a good story now?" he said, sitting back down and telling his facial muscles to work his mouth into the shape of a smile.

"Pretty near," I said, with a smile I hoped was better than his. "I was still wondering about this Glen, though. Did you ever meet him yourself, Earl?"

"I met him, sure. Rodney does the diving mostly, and I do the business side."

"But he paid Earl directly, out on the boat?"

"Yeah, but that's only part of it. You got to figure out how much to charge, keep the books, that kind of stuff. Earl, here, he'd go out and do jobs for practically nothing if he didn't have a certain party to negotiate for him."

"So you met with Glen to talk about the job, decide on a price? How did he strike you?"

"Not too bad a guy. Don't talk much."

"I think maybe I saw him once," I said. "Bald guy? Big mustache?"

"That's him."

"He knows boats?"

"Oh, yeah. Real good."

"Looks more like a weight lifter than a sailor."

"Ayuh, he's wicked strong."

"When I saw him I thought maybe security. A body-guard, something like that."

"Well, I wouldn't want to fuck with him. You wouldn't fuck with him, would you, Rodney?"

"Shit, no."

"So maybe he is a bodyguard," I said.

"But he's a sailor, too," Earl said. "Does the work. Keeps that boat looking good, don't he, Rodney?"

"Like a baby."

"Listen, we paid up here?" Earl said. "Because I got something out in the car I want to show you."

"Okay," I said. I didn't ask what it was because I've been invited out to lots of parking lots in lots of places like Captain Billy's, and I figured I knew what Earl wanted to show me. Or rather what he had told Rodney to show me. Earl struck me as more of an executive than a hands-on guy.

A car was just pulling away when we got out to the

parking lot, but then we were alone. I let Earl take me over to a three-toned clunker not far from my own clunker. The original paint on his was pea soup green, the body cancer was rust-colored, and the spots of primer were gray. "Your car?" I said, making note of the plate number just in case.

"One of them," Earl said. The only one not up on cinder blocks in his yard, probably.

"Good automobiles," I said. "Those Novas."

"Shut the fuck up. Listen, Henderson, you're no more of a goddamn reporter than I am. What are you?"

"You saw my press card."

"Fuck your press card. How come you want to know all about money and bodyguards?"

"For my story."

"Fuck your story. You tell me who you really are or Rodney stomps the shit out of you."

"Don't do that. Listen, guys, I really am a reporter."

Rodney had been in prison, so he had probably at least learned not to go through the usual male dance of aggression, pushing and shoving and shouting back and forth. He'd go for the sucker punch.

"One more chance, asshole," Earl said.

"Listen, please. What did I ever do to . . ."

In midsentence I shot for Rodney's legs. First of all, people never expect you to interrupt yourself. Second, only a wrestler expects your first move to be a grab for his knees. I upended Rodney onto his back, figuring that he wouldn't know how to break his fall. He didn't. The smack of 250 or so pounds hitting the blacktop shook him loose from his senses for the seconds it took me to lever him over onto his belly and bend his right leg back on itself. His old gray running shoe, size thirteen or so, almost came off during the operation. He had no socks on, which gave me an idea.

Earl was standing by, but not in range. He started to back toward his car. "Whatever you got in the car," I said, "don't get it. You do, and I'll shove it right up your skinny ass. Promise."

Earl stopped. I took Rodney's shoe all the way off, grabbed hold of his big toe, and stood up. Rodney was getting things back into focus, but he still just lay there on his belly like a beached walrus, looking back at me over his shoulder.

"Get him," Earl shouted. "Kill the fucker."

Rodney made a little movement, starting to roll over, but then he cried out and stopped.

"Go on," Earl said. He sounded like he might be about to cry. "What's the matter with you? Get up!"

"He can't. I got his toe. Want to see him turn over?"

Rodney screamed when I twisted my grip, and then turned over on his back to keep the toe I held from breaking. I twisted again and he completed the 360, back onto his belly again.

"What are you doing to him?"

"See now, you're learning something, Earl. You get a guy by the big toe, you can make him roll over by just twisting. Watch. Roll, Rodney. That's it, big fella. Roll."

I'd sooner have had Earl down there, but I made do with what I had. I just pictured Rodney holding that girl while Earl attacked her, and I was happy. "Roll, Rodney," I sang out. "Roll! Good boy."

Rodney was rolling and rolling now, in a big circle with me at the center. A man came out of the bar with two women. They stopped, keeping a safe distance.

"You know Rodney?" I called out, and they nodded. "Want to see him roll? Roll, Rodney." They looked at Rodney rolling, they looked at Earl standing by, they looked at me, not understanding how I was making the local tough guy squeal and roll around in a circle. They didn't want to stay and they didn't want to go.

"I'm going to let him loose in a minute and he'll probably be pretty pissed off," I said. "Maybe you better go on home."

When they had driven off, I let Rodney go.

"You fucker," Earl said.

"Yeah," I said. "Right."

And I got in my car, too, and drove off. As I headed back to the campground, I wondered why Earl and Rodney would know so much about Billene Somerville's shopping habits in Camden. You had to be asking around and following people to learn stuff like that. Why would they be so curious? And why would they want to hammer on a stranger who was curious about the same things?

10

THERE WAS NO MORE THAN A sliver of moon, not enough to dim the stars. Probably it was too early in the year and too cool for bugs; at least there were none for the moment. I was tempted to pull my mattresses out of the tent and sleep under the stars, and might have done it if I had been off in the woods alone. But I was in a campground. Maybe I'd wake up next morning and find that kids had been gaping at me while I had been gaping, too, and possibly even drooling a little onto the pillow. After all, a man has his pride. I crawled inside the tent.

There I zipped myself up inside the nylon netting, in case the mosquitoes came out later on, and got out of my clothes. I put on old sweats, which are the perfect pajamas for camping. A blanket on top of me would make me just warm enough. My two foam mattresses and my two pillows, and I was more comfortable than home in bed.

I lay awake for a few minutes, though, thinking about the night. The *Billene*, a hole in the water into which you throw money. Did she go around the Caribbean during the winter, stopping at offshore banks for money to throw in her? Is that what was happening to the millions that Somerville skimmed from his operation, and Harmon H. Harmon stashed for him day after day? What sharks were circling around the hole in the water now, besides me? Earl and Rodney, more than likely. How about Glen, the man Rodney was so afraid of?

Rodney wouldn't have had the brains to think of teaming up with Billene's watchdog, but Earl might have. Which was why I had asked him if he had ever met Glen. He had, and so the two of them would have had the opportunity to reach an understanding. If they were in it together, though, why had Earl and Rodney talked to me at all? Besides, why would Glen want to go in with anybody else? If there were money to steal, he'd be in a position to do it all alone. Of course, that would leave him as the lone suspect, too. Dr. Potter and Hostetter wouldn't bother to worry about formal proof. Suppose Glen *was* in with the Thornburghs? Then he might be able to pluck Billene clean and blame it on the two of them. Having done what to keep them quiet? Disappeared them somehow?

Complicated.

Keep it simple. What do you know for sure? Nothing much. Just that there's enough money aboard for Billene to pay her bills in cash. And that questions along those lines got a couple of local burglars angrier than the situation seemed to call for.

All of which a psychiatrist would call projection. I was circling in the water my own self, and so naturally I was starting to see all the other fish as sharks, too . . .

I was almost asleep when a sound brought me awake.

A bump of some kind, maybe. I hadn't been awake enough to classify it. But the next sound was somebody saying shush. Late arrivals. At least they hadn't driven in with their lights on and started slamming doors. Why not? Why hadn't I heard their car? A scratch sounded, the noise only a match makes. A little flare of light was just visible through the thin fabric of the tent, moving. The match?

"Gotta be his tent," a voice whispered. "That was his car."

"I told you he wasn't no reporter," another voice whispered. "Fucking reporters stay in a hotel, not in no fucking tent. Knock it down."

Oh, shit.

The tent flap was down by my feet. I had just made it there, and was on all fours fumbling at the zipper that closed the nylon mosquito netting, when I heard a voice whisper, "Watch this." Then came running steps, then somebody huge and heavy fell on me and smashed me flat. I moved automatically to escape from under, but of course I couldn't, not with the tent collapsed around me. Then the weight was gone and the beating began.

Blinded and helpless in the straitjacket of my tent, I twisted to escape. "Roll, motherfucker, roll," Earl kept saying, grunting each time as he hit me with something hard and heavy. Rodney was grunting, too, but not wasting breath on talk. He was using his feet, stomping and kicking.

Earl was the one to worry about, with his jack handle or whatever it was. The first blow from it had hit the side of my head. There's no pain right when you're first hit, but you know when real damage has been done. The system is shocked. You want to just lie there. You don't, though, if you've had it drilled into you long enough that to stop moving is to lose. I rolled, like he said, and the next blow didn't hurt so much. In my struggle I had wound up with one of the foam mattresses partly over me, and it softened the blow. I did my best to keep under it while the beating and the kicking went on. Both men were grunting with the effort of their blows, and a couple times there was a clank when Earl's weapon hit one of the aluminum tubes that used to keep up the tent.

At least I hadn't been zipped up in a sleeping bag, but I was still trapped in the large, loose bag made by the tent. I couldn't grab, couldn't hit, couldn't get away from the blows long enough to find the zipper in the dark and free myself. Whether he meant to kill me or not, Earl might brain me any minute with his steel bar. The only thing left to do was to make noise, so I shouted for help as loud as I could. Rodney was gasping for breath from his kicking and stomping, but Earl managed to snarl, "Shut the fuck up." I shouted all the harder next time the bar hit me.

A dog started to bark.

"Come on, let's get the fuck out of here," Rodney wheezed. He had stopped kicking.

"You're lucky, motherfucker," Earl said. "We catch you around here again, we'll fucking kill you next time." He brought his bar down on me again, and grunted with the effort.

"Yeah," Rodney said. "Find your own fucking jobs."

"Will you shut the fuck up, Rodney?"

"He already knows, don't he, Earl? You said so."

"Never mind what I said. Let's get going, I hear somebody."

I kept shouting for a minute, but they weren't hitting me anymore so I stopped. I could hear them stumbling through the woods, but I couldn't hear anybody else. After a while I heard the noise of a car starting, far enough away so that they must have parked just off Route 1 and walked in.

I found the zipper at last, and worked the tent open. My first thought, close to a hysterical one, was to get free of my trap. I thrashed in panic when I got tangled for a moment in the narrow opening I had made, and I could hear the nylon netting tear. As soon as I had kicked free I crawled frantically away, and only calmed down when I thumped my head into a tree in the dark. Earl had clubbed me in just the same spot, and the new pain was white hot on top of the old. When the sudden, sharp agony began to ease, I became aware of how much I hurt everywhere else, too. I realized, also, that the right side of my head, where I had taken Earl's first and most damaging blow, was wet. I hoped it wasn't coming from the ear. Blood from the ear could be serious stuff.

I tried to think in spite of the pain and the overwhelming desire just to curl up and whimper. Rodney and Earl probably wouldn't come back tonight, but they might very likely check next morning to see if my car was gone. I didn't want to draw any attention to myself, which meant getting out of the campgrounds before the manager saw the state I was in. But I still had plans for the *Billene*, and now I had plans for the Thornburgh boys, too. They could easily have killed me. They might even have been trying to. Rodney, at least, was dumb enough—and certainly mad enough.

I needed first off to find a safe place where I could obey my body, and curl up while I healed. Bent over like an old man, I took it step by step back to the tent. The bedding and my clothes were inside. I slowly dragged the collapsed tent over to the car. The aluminum frame that had softened some of the blows was bent and ruined, but the rods came apart all right. The damned zipper on the mosquito net had jammed, so I couldn't remove the foam mattresses that had very likely saved my life. I had to shove the whole mess all together into the back seat of the Datsun, like cramming a couple of pillows into a single pillowcase. I had forgotten the camp chair, but the hell with it. It wasn't worth the pain of hobbling back.

On the drive back down to Lincolnville I had to pull over once, to lean out of the door and vomit. That scared me a little. I had been hurt plenty before, but never to the point where I had to vomit. In Lincolnville, I pulled into the parking lot of the lobster pound. From there I could watch the ferry line forming and join it once a few cars were in front of me and I wouldn't stand out. Blood makes you stand out, too, so I forced myself down to the waterfront and washed my face clean. The sweatshirt was navy blue and didn't matter; the stains wouldn't show on it for what they were. And it had a hood, which would cover the caked blood that matted the right side of my head. As far as I could tell by probing with my fingers, the blood came from a tear in the flesh where the jack handle had ripped my ear partway loose from my head. It was a relief to know I wasn't bleeding from inside the ear.

Back in the car, I sat down to hurt, and to wait for daylight. The first ferry for Islesboro didn't leave till eight.

My strength was pretty nearly gone by the time I got to Felicia's house. I managed to unlock the barn door, drive inside, relock the door after me, let myself in the house, and make it upstairs to the front bedroom. I didn't care that all my gear was back out in the car, or that the newspapers still covered the nearest bed. I fell right on top of them.

The room faced east and was just getting dark when

I finally came awake. My watch showed a little after seven, so that I had been asleep more than ten hours. I felt absolutely terrible, worse than before. My injuries had stiffened up, so that any movement at all caused pain. But I could move, anyway. Thanks to the foam mattresses, nothing was broken, although everything was bruised.

In baby steps I made it to the bathroom and looked at myself in the fading light. My right eye was black from the blow that had come close to tearing my ear off, but otherwise my face was all right except for the smudges of printer's ink from sleeping ten hours on the *Bangor Daily News*. I didn't want to face the pain involved in taking my sweatshirt off, but at least I lifted it up. Dark bruises stood out on my ribs, my stomach, and over my kidneys. Pain told me there would be others all over my legs, my back, my arms, and my shoulders. My hands weren't hurt, and neither was one foot. But Earl must have got me on the other foot with his jack handle or tire iron. A kick from one of Rodney's rubber-soled shoes couldn't have caused as much damage as there was to my left heel.

My mouth was foul from last night's vomit, and the faucet on the sink came up dry. It was even worse than that, I knew, when I saw that the toilet bowl was dry, too. The plumber hadn't come by yet to get the system ready for summer. There was no water. I hobbled down-stairs, keeping the weight off my injured heel, to see if I could find something to drink. I did, but it was a large can of tomato juice. The idea of rinsing my mouth out with tomato juice was disgusting, but it was the only idea I could come up with. So I went out onto the back stoop and did it, looking like I was puking blood. Then I locked myself back inside the house and carried the rest of the tomato juice back upstairs with me. After a while I was able to get some of it down. By now the light was gone and there was nothing to do but go to bed again. This time I did it right. I pulled the newspapers off onto the floor and replaced them with a couple of blankets and pillows from the chest of drawers.

I slept badly, the way you do on stony ground, half-waking throughout the night and turning to find a position that hurts less. But when I woke up all the way, it was the sound of a car door closing that did it. Then came voices. I started out of bed just as if I wasn't half-crippled, but the pain told me better. I hobbled like an old man over to the window and looked between the curtains at the same plumber's truck I had seen in Dark Harbor on my first reconnaissance. The plumber and his helper were just heading toward the house, carrying tools.

Myself, I went over to the bedroom door and locked it. Then I went back to bed. No reason I could think of why the bedroom door shouldn't have been left locked, and no reason why a plumber would want to come into a bedroom anyway. For a while the two of them made various noises downstairs. When they came upstairs to tend to the bathroom across the hall, I could make out what they were saying.

"Don't look too bad, does it?" said a voice that belonged to the plumber, from the middle-aged sound of it.

"Not too," said a younger voice, the helper.

"Leaks some, though. She'll swell up after a while, but better run down to the kitchen and get a pot to put under for now."

When the helper came back up with the pot, he said, "You know Harvey Beckwith from Camden, don't you? Works maintenance over to the inn? I come over with him on the boat this morning, turns out he was one of the ones that actually seen Rodney Thornburgh get whipped."

"That right?"

"Ayuh. Harvey and a couple girls, they came out when the fellow had Rodney already on the ground."

"That true, that he had him by the great toe?"

"According to what Harvey says. Says the guy was twisting Rodney's toe, saying roll, Rodney, roll, Rodney, like that."

"And Rodney rolled, did he?"

"According to what Harvey said, yes."

"I'd like to have seen that."

"Me, too," the assistant said. "Particularly as it was Rodney. Wicked big pile of shit to roll."

"What was Earl supposed to have been doing all this time?"

"Just standing there. You know Earl, all he does is egg Rodney on."

"They know who the fellow is?"

"Lou that tends bar, all he knows is he talked like a tourist."

"We can use that kind of tourist. Ought to give him a goddamned medal."

"Lobstermen's association could make one up," the helper said.

"People he busted into their homes, they might pitch in too."

"Plenty of girls around, they'd help."

"What girls is that?"

"Well, not mentioning any names, I've heard that Earl and Rodney can get pretty rough sometimes."

"Good thing we run Rodney off the island. Let Belfast worry about him."

"How'd you folks manage that, anyway?"

"Things kept happening to his boat, his cars. Nobody wouldn't hire him. Nobody wouldn't talk to him. I guess he figured he'd be more comfortable somewhere folks didn't know him so good."

"In Camden, we know him as good as we want to."

"I can imagine. Well, you got everything shipshape there, Luther? We about done in here?"

"You said remind you to turn the water heater on."

"Good for you. I'm reminded."

"They coming up this early, then?"

"Not till June, but I turn it on now just to save coming over and doing it later."

"It's just throwing a switch."

"He's a bishop and she's a poet. The two of them together wouldn't have enough sense to change a light bulb."

Now I'd be able to take a hot bath. It wouldn't make me heal any faster, but I'd feel better for as long as I was in the tub, and I'd be able to soak some of the caked blood out of my hair. Once the noise of the plumber's truck had disappeared, I picked up a John D. McDonald from among the books piled on the bedside tables and got busy waiting for the water in the tank downstairs to heat up.

After a few pages, though, it struck me that I might as well do this bath right. My razor and toothbrush were out in the barn, along with clothes that hadn't been slept in and bled on for the last couple of nights. I raised myself to a sitting position, moved my feet carefully off the bed, put them carefully on the floor, and even more carefully assumed a semierect position. It took two trips to carry everything I needed back inside, and the two trips, in my state, took long enough for the water to heat up. I thought of old people with things like gout, bursitis, osteoporosis, arthritis—folks sentenced to live the rest of their lives like this. I admired them, but I also wondered why they bothered to summon up the courage to go on.

Well, I was going on, wasn't I, when I could have stood in bed? And doing it for no better reason than personal hygiene. After half an hour in the tub, I went back to bed where I belonged. I got up only to feed myself. For lunch I just had smoked almonds, feeling good about being able to pig out on a whole can all at once. But by suppertime I was seriously hungry. Along with lots of other stuff, as I was glad to find out, Felicia had a couple of old gallon jars with macaroni stored in them. It was in designer shapes, but probably it was just as good as regular noodles. She had a big selection of canned soups, too. Since this was Felicia's kitchen, I knew she had to have a supply of the essential ingredient somewhere. So I kept looking till I found a half-full commercial-sized bottle of Tabasco sauce. It had turned that disgusting tan color that comes from sitting around open for a year or so, but you don't have to worry about Tabasco sauce rotting on you. It's rotted when you buy it. That's what gives it the flavor that time can't kill.

Once the macaroni was boiled up soft I poured off the water and moved ahead with my recipe. The trick at this stage is to make a little hole in one end of a can of soup so as to break the suction. Then when you remove the other end, the condensed mushroom slides right out like a nice, neat core sample and you don't have to grub around inside the can for the last little bits. I busted the cylinder of soup up with a wooden spoon and stirred it around in the hot macaroni till the lumps got small. Then a lot of black pepper and a heavy hit of Tabasco sauce, and I was ready to start stoking.

I put away the whole potful, which I took to be a sign that the system was on the mend and needed plenty of material to work with. I didn't feel sleepy yet, so I went upstairs and moved my bedding from the front bedroom to one of the rear ones. That way I could turn the light on and read without attracting attention from the road. But I hadn't read more than a couple of pages before I passed out. I woke up around midnight with the light still on and the open book beside me. I closed the book, put out the light, and didn't come to again until daybreak.

Without the pain, the rest of the week would have been the perfect vacation. I was parked in the middle of a huge pile of books and blankets and pillows, with nobody even knowing where I was, let alone bothering the house guest to see that he was having a good time. Mostly, I was.

During the days I'd move my operation to the front bedroom, where I could keep an eye on the *Billene* whenever I thought of it. One time they went out in the dinghy, if you can use the word for a boat as fancy as the *Billene*'s launch. They had rods, and when they came back Glen spent a while cleaning fish on the diving platform at the rear of the yacht. They were bluefish or mackerel from the shape of them, although it was too far to tell which. I wondered if he did the cooking aboard, or if she did. I wondered about their life in general. He worked out every day on deck, and did small jobs there now and then, but most of the time he was down below. Billene spent most of her time down there, too.

Presumably the last couple of years had gone along pretty much the same way, at least when they were in port. It was hard to believe that their relationship was strictly professional, and yet what did I know? Maybe Glen was silent, unobtrusive, deferential, polite, self-effacing—the perfect servant. But, watching him at his workouts, it was a lot easier to picture Glen as a cell block boss than as a butler.

When there was nothing to see aboard the *Billene*, which was most of the time, I read or did workouts of my own. Workouts are never much fun, and anyone who thinks they are just isn't doing them right. Done properly, a productive session is usually boring and frequently painful. The only thing approaching a rush comes when you're finally finished.

And what I was doing was even less fun than my normal routine. It was pure rehab therapy, where the object is to cause yourself pain in exchange for a little gain. First I'd try to loosen up, which meant forcing my bruised bones, tendons, sinews, and muscles to go places they didn't want to go. Eventually I'd be a little looser than before, maybe, but still pretty knotted up. Then I'd do like Glen—slow repetitions of various isotonic exercises, trying for perfect form and a full range of movement. But where Glen was going for the burn, I did only enough to pump blood into the muscles. Blood is the great healer, and the more of it you get to an injury, the better. My old team trainer at Iowa taught me that. For all I know he may have been right.

In any event, I kept at it throughout the day, off and on. And then the next day and the next, and each day it hurt just a little bit less. After a week I was still stiff and sore, but I could move almost normally. The bruises had faded, and my clothes covered all but one of them. My hair covered that one, which was where Earl had landed his first shot with the tire iron or jack handle, or whatever it was. The spot was still swollen and tender, but the huge knot above my right ear was mostly gone. A thick scab covered the wound where my ear had started to tear loose from my head. There would be a scar, but you'd have to look behind the ear to see it.

The thought of the scar didn't bother me. Wrestlers live with the prospect of ugly ears. My own never cauliflowered, but I'm surprised they didn't and wouldn't care much if they had. That's the club I joined.

The main thing wrong with me now was my heel, which I still had to favor. Unlike the ear, this did bother me. Heels get lots of pounding just in the course of everyday living, so that heel pain has a way of becoming chronic. I might have to give up running. And in general I had been hurt worse than ever before in my life—bone-deep pain all over my body. I had felt the terrifying sensation of total, childlike impotence, when I had been blind and helpless and effectively limbless inside the unbreakable shroud of my tent.

And these were the things that made me push myself so hard and painfully through the recovery process. I couldn't wait to sit down and reason with Earl and Rodney Thornburgh. I felt the same way my father would feel when he'd haul his drunken ass home after somebody or other had once again whipped it for him.

"I'll get them fuckers, see if I don't," he'd start hollering while he was still staggering up the drive. We'd all scatter, so he wouldn't get us instead. "I'll take them fuckers apart piece by piece and send them back to Jesus."

11

To find Rodney and Earl
Thornburgh, all I had to do was get to Captain Billy's
Saloon a little before closing time and wait down the
street for them to come out. They headed for Earl's Nova
and left the parking lot with tires squealing. Probably
Earl had learned from cop movies that it's bad form to
drive off in a car without making a cool noise, no matter
whether you're in a hurry or not. I stayed well back of
him while we were still in town, but then I closed the
distance till my high beams were near enough to irritate
him. He could try to outrun me, which most likely
wouldn't work. My clunker didn't look any better than
his clunker, but his puked black smoke out the tail pipe
and mine was in perfect mechanical condition. Or he
could pull over in hopes I would stop so the two of
them could beat the shit out of me. In which case I
would educate them right there beside the road.

Or Earl could just lead me to home, which is what he

did. A couple of miles out of town, the brake lights went on and the car turned off the road going much too fast. I hoped he would lose it so that a tree would bust him up and save me the trouble, but he managed to keep the Nova on all four wheels as it disappeared into the woods. I blew on by, doing about sixty-five until I was around a couple of bends. Then I made a U-turn, pulled off onto the shoulder, cut my lights, and waited till my eyes got used to seeing in the moonlight.

I didn't meet any other cars as I drove slowly back, trying to find where Earl had left the road. I would have missed it if I hadn't spotted light through the trees, twenty or thirty yards back from the highway. The question was what to do—go in after them or try to get them outside somehow. Outside might be better. Earl wouldn't be much to worry about without a weapon, but inside he might be able to put his hands on one. Outside I could just disable him fast and then go for Rodney.

In a minute Earl solved the problem, or at least a Nova came out of the driveway with only one head visible in the front seat. It hadn't occurred to me that Earl might live somewhere else and just be dropping off his cousin. The car turned in the other direction from where I was parked and went off down the road. Life had just become simple.

I drove into the dirt driveway with the headlights still off, although it didn't really matter much. If he didn't hear me come in, fine. If he did, he'd probably just think it was Earl coming back. The house was a rusting trailer that hadn't moved an inch for thirty years. There were a hundred just like it tucked off the highways around my hometown in upstate New York, and I wouldn't have needed the light from the trailer windows to tell me what the yard was like: junk, old tires, an old F1 Ford pickup with the windshield busted out, a discarded washing machine, tangles of rusty barbed wire, a pipe cutter standing on its steel legs. The only thing new and unbent and rust-free was a satellite dish rising up out back.

All of this, including the three-thousand-dollar dish, was standard lawn furniture for the rural slum that covers most of America with ugly little patches like this one. Because the patches aren't all together in one spot, and because a lot of them are hidden from the road, people think of poverty as a black, urban problem. But most poor folks are white, and most of them live in and around little towns just like the ones Reagan grew up in. And the one Bush vacations in, come to think of it. Maine is the poorest state in New England, one of the poorest in the nation.

I knew Rodney would have dogs, and I suspected they'd be hunting dogs, kept caged up. And there they were, jumping up against the chicken wire of their pen and barking insanely even before I got out of the car. I didn't want to give Rodney a chance to think things over, so I went straight up to the door and hammered on it.

"Shut the fuck up, you fuckers," Rodney hollered through the door to his dogs. "It ain't nobody but fucking Earl." As soon as the door moved, I put a shoulder to it hard enough to knock Rodney off his feet. He was on his back when I burst in, not hurt but startled.

"Hi," I said. "It's me."

He focused on where he was, and who I was. "It was all Earl's idea, mister," he said. It was a promising beginning.

"Earl gets you in a lot of shit, doesn't he?"

"Maybe."

"He got you in some real deep shit this time. This time you don't just go to jail. This time you get your arms broken, then your legs. I'm going to fuck up one of your knees, too, so you limp the rest of your life. They can't set knees. You know that, Rodney? Talk to me, Rodney."

He didn't want to talk. He rolled over and tried to get up to come at me, but he was drunk and he didn't move too well. I used to do the kicking on my high school football team, and I gave him about a sixty-yard punt, right in the face. It raised him up from his hands and knees, big as he was, and dumped him on his back again. His mouth was ruined, and blood was pouring from his nose. I kneeled down beside him.

"You like to kick people, don't you? There's some kicking for you."

He tried to speak, but it sort of bubbled. He tried again, and this time I made it out. He was saying, "I give up, I give up." Rodney had gone back in his head, all the way back to the playground. He didn't want me to give him any more noogies.

"I don't give a fuck if you give up, Rodney. We're not doing games here. We're doing payback here."

Rodney shook his head, slow and dumb as a cow.

"You don't want me to hurt you anymore?"

His head kept shaking back and forth. Now blood was coming from his mouth, too. It soaked the front of his shirt. I didn't want to touch the mess I had made of him, but I would. Rodney knew that.

"Please," he said. "Please." I might have felt sorry for him, except that I knew he'd filet me and leave me to die with my guts in my lap if he had the chance.

"Please, what? You got to pay me back for what you did to me, Rodney."

He shook his head even faster, no, no, no.

"Well, maybe if you talk to me, I won't do your knee. The rest of what I do, it'll all heal up eventually." I went over to the sink, ran water on a dirty towel till it was soaking, and threw it at him. "Get the blood out of your fucking mouth and see if you can talk."

Rodney got up slowly, looking at me all the while as if he was asking permission, and went over to the sink. While he cleaned up I stayed near enough to make sure he didn't get into the knife drawer or something.

"Stuff some of that paper towel up your nose," I said. "You're running like a faucet."

When he had done it, the paper plugs turned red right away. But they seemed to stop the flow.

"You look like a roast pig, Rodney, you know that?" I said. "Only you got the cherries in your snout instead of your eyes."

I gestured toward an armchair that looked like he had shortstopped it on its way to the dump. "Sit," I said. "SIT!"

He sat. I looked around for the right thing for the job and found it. "What you doing?" Rodney mumbled when I unplugged the twenty-seven-inch Zenith that had probably put him in hock for eight hundred bucks, on top of the payments for the dish outside. I didn't answer, just staggered over with the TV and set it down in his lap.

"Hold on tight," I said, pretty sure that he would. I figured he couldn't possibly let something that lovely fall to the floor, no matter how badly he might want to get up and go after me. And it was much too heavy to throw.

"Earl has been jacking you around for years," I said. "What do you think? Think he's jacking you around again, Rodney?"

"What do you mean?"

"Figure it out. You do all the work the way you always do. Then him and this guy Glen, next thing you know they're in Mexico or some goddamned place and you're back where you usually are. Jail."

"That's bullshit."

"Yeah, well, my point is, how do you know? Supposing I came to you a few years back, I said to you, Rodney, you're going to take a couple of little vacations down in Thomaston. On the other hand, Earl here, he's going to hang around Captain Billy's, shooting bumper pool and dipping his wick into girls instead of boys. I bet you would have said that was bullshit, too."

Rodney didn't make any answer.

"Only it wasn't bullshit, was it? Look, Earl was the guy that talked business with this Glen while you did the real work. You think all they talked about was estimates, invoices, that crap? Get real, Rodney. They were setting this deal up behind your back."

"You don't know as much as you think you do."

"Fill me in."

"Me and Earl are partners."

"Right. You do the heavy lifting, he answers the phone and sweeps up. Like in this deal now. Earl holds your coat, while you take out Glen."

"That's how much you know. One person couldn't take out Glen."

"How about me?"

"Even you. You ain't seen Glen."

"Tell me about him."

"He looks like that guy that worked for Nixon, what's his name? Bald guy? Big mustache?"

"G. Gordon Liddy?" All the time I was watching Glen through the glasses, he had reminded me of somebody. But I couldn't think who.

"Liddy, yeah. Only wicked strong. Plenty of them guys down at Thomaston, think they're tough, all right? Well, those guys they wouldn't never fuck with Glen."

"Glen was at Thomaston?"

"That ain't what I mean. I just mean if those guys saw a guy like Glen around, they wouldn't fuck with him. Actually Glen was in jail somewhere, only not Thomaston."

"He tell you that?"

"His tattoos is what told me."

"Lot of guys have tattoos."

"Not like his. I seen them before once, on a guy that used to be in Huntsville."

"Huntsville they got a special tattoo?"

"Not special for Huntsville, no. Special for the Aryan Brotherhood."

I thought about that. Huntsville was the big Texas penitentiary, so that might fit. But Glen had been hired through Sunbelt Security Services. Would a former FBI man like E. R. Hostetter hire an ex-con? Probably depend on the crime. A guy who bombed synagogues or ran guns to fascist death squads, Hostetter might figure he was a prisoner of conscience who deserved a break.

"So the guys at Thomaston wouldn't fuck with Glen, and you wouldn't fuck with Glen," I said. "Okay, who *was* going to fuck with him?"

"I didn't say anybody was going to fuck with him."

"Rodney, when you two assholes got finished trying to beat my head in, you said I should stay out of your business. What's that supposed to mean? I shouldn't bust into summer houses?"

"Didn't mean nothing."

"What you said was I should find my own fucking jobs, Rodney. Then Earl said shut up. Then you said words to the effect of what's the difference, Earl? The guy already knows. So Rodney, here's the question. What was I supposed to already know?"

"I was just fucking talking, all right?"

"I was just fucking breaking your nose a few minutes ago. I had my nose broken a couple times. Hurts like a son of a bitch, am I right? What if I broke it again, Rodney? Broke it right on top of breaking it already?"

"You wouldn't do that."

"Hey, after what you fuckers did to me? I don't give a shit what I do to you. I want to do things to you, Rodney. You got to understand that. The only way I'm not going to bust your nose again is a little cooperation here. You understand?"

Rodney nodded.

"That's it. You just nod when I get something right. That way you can tell anybody that asks that you never said a word. All right. I come around asking a lot of questions about Mrs. Somerville and they don't sound to you like reporter questions, am I right?"

He nodded.

"In fact they're mostly money questions, so you figure I'm interested in whether there's money on board?"

I was right again.

"And so Earl takes you out to the can and tells you to stomp me a little?" Another nod. "When that doesn't work out, you follow my car or you spot the camping stuff in the back and that tells you where to find me. You know there's only one campground open this early. Now the question is, why would you want to stomp me in the parking lot? Because you thought I wanted to rob that yacht?"

Rodney nodded.

"Why would you give a shit if I wanted to rob a yacht, Rodney? What are you guys, the fucking Coast Guard?"

This time he didn't mind answering out loud. "Them fucks," he said.

"Yeah, right. Okay, all we've got left here is that the only reason you'd possibly give a shit is because you're about to rob it yourself. That's the job you were talking about. Am I right on this, Rodney?"

Rodney's big head didn't move.

"Whatever," I said, starting toward him. He flinched, and nodded.

"Okay, fine. We're in business then. Earl got a phone?"

"Sure he's got a phone."

So did Rodney. It looked like it had cost him $19.95 at Radio Shack a long time ago. I carried it over to Rodney and said, "Call him."

"What do I tell him?"

"Tell him you've got a busted mouth and a busted nose, but you'll recover. Tell him to come over, that he was right about me, I'm not a reporter. Tell him I'm a thief just like you, and we've got business to talk. Tell him I'm coming in on this thing or it doesn't happen. Because I'll go to Glen and tell him what you guys are up to. Tell him all those things."

Rodney told him. I had to take the phone myself after a while and do a little reassuring, but finally Earl agreed to come over. He said it would take ten minutes or so, not more than fifteen.

"You got a gun?" I asked Rodney after I hung up on his cousin.

Rodney thought about that for a moment, although he had to know the right answer by heart. "No," he said.

"Come on, Rodney, you got a couple of hounds out there. What do you do when they scare up a rabbit or something? Choke it to death?"

"Gun's busted. It's over to Belfast, in the shop."

"Whatever you say, Rodney. I'll just have to look around for it. Only when I find it, I'll smack you in the mouth with the fucking thing."

"It's in the back of the closet."

It turned out to be a 12-gauge Remington pump gun.

I checked the load, which was double-aught buckshot, and closed up the gun again. I checked the safety.

"Off is when the red's showing, right?" I asked him.

"Why? What are you going to do to me?"

"Nothing. We're partners. But Earl probably doesn't really understand that yet."

Earl drove up about when he said he would. The dogs barked at him, too, the way they had at me. He spent a minute or so sitting in his car, probably looking the situation over. But there wasn't much to see, just a trailer with light coming out of it. I heard the car door slam, and heard the dogs go even crazier once he headed toward the trailer. "Tell him come on in, it's unlocked," I said from the bedroom. I would be out of sight from the front door, but I had a clear view of Rodney in his chair. A clear shot, too.

"Come on in, it's unlocked," Rodney hollered when he heard his cousin at the door. I heard Earl push the door open, but he didn't come through it.

"You all right?" he said.

"Fuck no," Rodney said. "Look at me."

"What you doing with that TV on you?"

"He told me keep it there."

"Where is he?"

"I'm in here. I've got a shotgun pointed right at Rodney's balls."

Rodney nodded vigorously.

"Come on in and sit down, Earl," I called out. "We got to talk."

"I ain't coming in. You take me for a fool?"

"Look, if I wanted to shoot Rodney I would have done it already. If I wanted to shoot you, I would have waited out there in the dark and done that, too."

"What's the gun for, then?"

"Because I figured you'd bring a gun. You don't know we're partners yet."

"I don't have no gun."

"Fine. Come in to where I can see you, and I'll unload mine. Ask Rodney. He'll tell you everything's going to be all right."

"I think maybe it is," Rodney said. The broken nose made him sound as if he had a bad cold. "He's right, he could have killed us already if he was going to. Don't you think, Earl? He could have, couldn't he?"

"Shut the fuck up, Rodney."

"Come on in, Earl," I said.

"I'm thinking about it." After a moment he said, "Okay, I'm coming in. Don't try no smart stuff."

As soon as I could see through the doorway that he had nothing in his hands, I said, "Take off your jacket and your shirt, will you?"

"I thought you was going to unload the gun."

"I am, as soon as I know you don't have one."

"Jesus, some partner you are." But he took off his jacket, and then his shirt. He was narrow chested and narrow shouldered. The tattoo of a screaming eagle on his stringy biceps looked silly.

"You were in the 101st?" I asked. That first night back in Captain Billy's, he had told me he was in the 25th Infantry.

"It's just a picture."

Which meant he knew it was the crest of the 101st Airborne Division. The only thing more pathetic than going airborne is not going airborne and getting an airborne tattoo instead.

"Now grab each pant leg at the knee and pull them up till I can see the top of your sock."

"What the fuck is this?"

"Just do it, Earl."

"Like fuck I will."

"Jesus, Earl. Which leg is it on?"

"It's my backup piece, man."

Backup piece. Thank God for TV, or petty thieves in Belfast, Maine, wouldn't know how to say really cool things like backup piece. I managed not to tell Earl what an asshole he was, though. After all, we were partners.

"Put your leg where Rodney can get to the goddamned thing. Take the gun out with your thumb and finger, Rodney, and toss it over by me. Come on, let's get going. We've got things to talk about."

When I had Earl's little chrome-plated .32-caliber pistol, I put it away with Rodney's shotgun in the bedroom. "All right," I said, "let's hear what you guys got in mind."

And actually it turned out to be a sound enough plan, although with a few weak spots that wouldn't be too much trouble to rethink. Once the Thornburgh boys were sober and rested. Meanwhile it was close to four, and time for even Rodney and Earl to go to bed.

"All right," I said, "we may as well get it over with as quick as we can get organized."

"We got till the end of the month. That's when they left last year."

"Yeah, well, we don't know for sure when they're going to leave this year. All we know for sure is that they're here now. The best thing is to go as soon as we're ready. I'll rent my equipment tomorrow."

"You won't need nothing," Rodney said "I got plenty of spare gear out back in the workshop."

"How about a wet suit? Won't yours be too big?"

"Maybe in the waist, but we ain't going to be in the water long enough for it to matter."

"I'll come by tomorrow afternoon, try it on."

"Where can we get in touch with you?" Earl asked.

"I'll be moving around. But I'll be by tomorrow, and if the gear fits, we can shoot for the night after."

The sky was starting to lighten behind me as I pulled into a big, anonymous Days Inn off Route 202 in Augusta. I had eased along the two-lane roads, taking nearly an hour for the trip. All the way, I was going over the probabilities and the possibilities. My major concern wasn't with the plan itself; it was the risk that Rodney and Earl might try to kill me before the plan even got under way. Got along without you before I met you, the song says. Gonna get along without you now.

But I didn't think they were that dumb. Dumb, yes, but not that dumb. They had been stalling around up till now because they weren't quite confident they could pull it off with just the two of them. With three, though, it would be a lock.

I registered as Elliott Abrams, paid for two nights in advance, hung the DO NOT DISTURB sign out, and set the alarm for two P.M. That would get me back in Belfast well before my two partners had to leave for their daily appointment with Captain Billy.

12

SEE IF THESE FIT," RODNEY said, handing me a pair of diving boots before answering my question. "Yeah, I went below deck a couple times. To take a dump, and the other time to use his tools to fix my regulator. It was drawing hard."

"Where do you keep tools in a boat like that? The engine room?"

"He's got a workbench in the weight room."

"What's a weight room?"

"A room where they got weights. Like in a gym."

"This is one of the cabins or something? They converted it to a gym?"

"Yeah, mostly. Over in the corner they got a little workbench with all the tools hung up on pegboard, everything new, real clean."

You couldn't say that about Rodney's work area. He never threw anything out, it looked like. Old steel tanks were rusting on the floor. Masks without face plate, or without straps, the rubber cracked with age. Old double-hose regulators, one of which was going to be mine. An old horse-collar buoyancy control device that probably leaked, since you store them inflated and this one was now flat. Wet suits, dry suits, hoods, gloves, fins, and belts were piled or strewn all over the floor. Dirty tools were cluttered on the top of a workbench hammered together out of salvaged boards and two-by-fours. Light came from a bare bulb at the end of an extension cord looped over a nail in one of the four-bys that held up the tin roof.

"Who uses the weights?" I asked, not mentioning that I had watched Glen working out on deck. I didn't want Earl and Rodney to know I had access to a house that overlooked the *Billene*. I didn't want anybody at all to be able to make any connection between Felicia and me.

"Looked like both of them did," Rodney said. "There was a rack of regular plates up to fifties and hundreds. Them nice ones, all chromed. And there was a set of them women's dumbbells too. Pink and shit like that. It was a regular little tiny gym. Slant board, bench, one of them mini Universals. Wall-to-wall carpet, mirrors on the walls. Nice."

"You didn't go in the bedrooms?"

"I looked in at the master bedroom, is all."

"Probably the bedrooms is where they'd keep any guns. His bedroom, I guess."

"Nah, probably the bridge."

"Why the bridge?"

"That's where you'd need them. Say you saw a shark or something."

"Is it normal to carry guns on a boat?"

"Boat like that?" Earl cut in. "Fucking A."

"Why?"

"Boat like that, could run you around a half-million dollars. Want a gun, wouldn't you?"

"For what? Pirates?"

"Happens every day, maybe more down in the Caribbean. Boat goes out and it never comes back. You think they all sink?"

"Something worth that much, you couldn't sell it, could you? Wouldn't you need papers?"

"You get her down to Panama or the Bahamas, they don't care about no papers."

The diving boots fit me all right. The seam had separated a little at the ankle of one, but not enough to be worth glueing. The wet suit fit, too, better than I thought it would have, given the size of Rodney's gut.

"I put on a lot of weight down at Thomaston," he had explained. "All that starch."

For a few seconds after getting into the ocean with this rig on, I'd feel like the *pétomane* when that first jet of icy water hit him. But with me it would be around my abdomen, not inside it. And after a few moments the water would warm up. I knew about Maine water inside wet suits because my scuba class the year before had made its training dives off Kittery Point, in April. Actually I had learned to scuba a long time before that, during R&R leaves in the warm waters of the Gulf of Thailand. But since those days every American's inalienable right to kill himself by stupidity has been gradually eroded. Now you need to take an approved course and get a certificate from the diving bureaucracy before a shop will fill your air tanks. Only then can you go out and kill yourself by stupidity.

"With the weight belt on it'll be okay," I said to Rodney. "Let's go down the checklist."

Checklists hadn't been a big part of the Thornburghs' lives up till now. They had operated pretty much on an ad hoc basis, and the list business had been my idea. They didn't really see the point, but they played along. My checklist was fairly close to the normal type you find in the back of diving manuals, but some things were missing and some were added. We wouldn't be dragging along a float with a diver's flag to mark our position, for instance. The whole point of diving in the first place was so that nobody on the *Billene* or on shore could mark our position. That was the point of diving after dark, too—so that the chance of anybody spotting our bubbles would be minimized practically to zero. Normally we would have taken along underwater torches for a night dive, but for the same reason these were also missing from the list. On it were a couple of nontraditional items, though: plastic hand ties for restraining prisoners. They looked like the ones you get with trash bags, only a lot heavier.

"Where do you go to get these things?" I asked Earl as I checked them off my list.

"Law enforcement catalogs."

Well, of course. Cops and robbers have the same consumer profile, and probably get the same catalogs.

"We all set, then?" I said when I had checked off everything on my list. "Tomorrow night at eleven-thirty?"

"Where can we reach you?" Earl asked.

"I'm still moving around."

"If something comes up and we got to call it off, though?"

"I'll know it's called off if you guys don't show," I said. "I'll get in touch, don't worry."

I caught the five o'clock ferry, the last of the day, over to Islesboro. This was the last time I'd be holing up there, if things went the way I planned, so I had stopped at a grocery in Belfast to replace the stuff I had eaten. I particularly replaced the old, brown Tabasco sauce—with two new bottles, still bright red, to show what a good house guest I was. For my last supper on the island, I got a quart of cream soda and a box of Nabisco Brown Edge Wafers. At rare intervals the mega-junk-food corporations get something just right and then have the sense to leave it alone. Brown Edge Wafers are an example. My intention was to hole up in Felicia's back bedroom, drink junk swill, eat junk food, read a junk book till I fell asleep in the crumbs, and then let my teeth rot till morning.

By morning, though, the feeling of decadence had passed and guilt set in. After brushing the fur out of my mouth, I thought about what I could do to minimize the effect of the cookies and cream soda. Running my four miles was out, since I didn't want to punish my injured heel to the point where it would never get better. I thought of Glen, on the deck of the *Billene*, and went to look for something I could use as a jump rope. I found a coil of clothesline out in the barn that did fine. As long as I stayed on my toes and off my heels, I had no problem except boredom. Which was pretty severe after twenty minutes of hopping up and down in the same place. Then I did the rest of Glen's exercise routine, as nearly as I could duplicate it. We might as well start out even.

The rest of the day I spent in the front bedroom, reading and spying on the motor yacht the same as I had during my recuperation. Actually I was still recuperating, a little. I still had some pain when I moved, but most of my wrestling career was spent in that state. You try to ignore it, although you don't entirely succeed. You wind up favoring the injury just a tiny bit, no matter how you try not to, and it's got to have some effect. But it shouldn't be enough to affect our plan, as long as Rodney had enough sense to do exactly what I told him. Rodney lacked skills, it was true, but so does an anchor. And all he had to be was an anchor.

Glen came out in midmorning to do his on-deck routine. Just after two o'clock he reappeared, this time with Billene. She wore a pink blouse and overalls. They were made on the same general model as Farmer Browns, with bib and shoulder straps and brass buttons no doubt, although it was too far to see. They had probably cost enough to pay for a half-dozen pairs of Sweet Orrs or Big Bens, though. Glen lowered the ship's boat, an operation I paid much closer attention to than I had the first time I watched him do it. The drill looked simple enough. He handed fishing gear down to Billene, and the two of them took off to catch some supper.

They came back in a couple of hours, apparently skunked. At least I didn't see them unload any fish, and Glen didn't come up on deck to do any fish cleaning later. Dusk fell, and the lights went on aboard the *Billene*. Probably Glen had recharged the boat's batteries during the fishing trip, so we wouldn't be able to count on generator noise to cover us as we boarded. But then we hadn't expected any different.

I sat at the window, looking across the bay at the light from the portholes and feeling nervous. I wondered if Earl and Rodney were feeling the same way. As experienced thieves, they ought to be used to it. But they might not be. I had broken into two different houses myself, and the second time didn't feel any better than the first. They had been empty houses, too. Come to think of it, so were the summer homes the Thornburgh cousins had burgled. The *Billene* wasn't empty, though, and a lot could go wrong. Our plan looked good to me, but if plans worked, every football play would be a touchdown. Five people were involved here, three on offense as you might say, and two on defense. Possibly two, anyway. For all we knew, Billene slept with an Uzi under the pillow.

Anyway for now there was nothing to do but breathe slowly from the diaphragm and wait for the action to start, like any other match. So I breathed slowly, and the time passed slowly, and at last it was quarter after ten. I got up to go. I wanted to be there early, watching from out of sight when Earl and Roy arrived.

I had taken a look at our meeting place yesterday evening, but now it was dark night with clouds moving in. I would have missed the drive leading to the place where the Thornburghs had stashed our gear if I hadn't counted steps on my first visit. The house had been 410 paces up the road from Felicia's, and on the ocean side of the road. I stepped over the chain across the drive, which probably would have tripped me if I hadn't seen it last evening. The drive was straight, and at the end of it was the pale reflection of the moon on Sabbathday Harbor. Then a patch of clouds moved across the moon, and all I could see was the sparkle of lights from the yacht, way out in the bay. The water was deep enough for Glen to have anchored much closer to shore, according to Rodney. It wasn't a good sign that he was some three hundred yards out. It argued that Glen routinely took steps to discourage visitors.

The moon came out again in a few minutes, so that I was able to find the hiding place I had settled on before. It was near the shed Rodney and Earl had theoretically broken into already. The idea had been for them to use bolt cutters on the padlock, store our gear, and then put their own padlock on the door. That way no one would stumble across our stuff and wonder what it was doing there. I lay down behind a little patch of blueberry bushes, with them between me and the shed. The bushes weren't even knee high, barely high enough to conceal a man lying down. There was plenty of better cover just as near the shed, but the best spot to hide is generally the least promising one. That's the last place people look.

The Thornburghs weren't due for nearly another hour, so I watched the only thing there was to watch, the lights on board the *Billene*. Would they be cooking? Reading? Playing cards? Listening to music? Watching TV? Together or in different cabins? The salon lights were on, but there were lights from below deck, too. First the salon lights went out, at quarter till eleven. Then, ten minutes later, the rest of the lights went out. The moon kept appearing and disappearing between the clouds, but the intervals between moonlight got longer. The rock I lay on was drawing heat out of me. The damp and chilly air didn't move much down where I was, but I could hear the treetops rustling a little. I was thoroughly uncomfortable, and wondering what had got into me to show up so early.

Earl and Rodney finally came, ten minutes early themselves. They made a good deal of noise coming down, and one of the cousins carried a flashlight, but it wouldn't matter. The house the shed belonged to was empty, and so were all the other houses along the road, on both sides. Seashore property was so expensive that most of the year-rounders lived inland.

"Tom?" Earl called out in a low voice.

"Fucker's not here yet," Rodney said.

" 'Course he's not here yet. We're early."

The beam moved around, stopping at the oil tank behind the house, the woodshed, the latticed space under the porch, and the hemlock hedge that probably marked the property line. It swept over my little, low blueberry patch without stopping. I wasn't more than ten yards from the shed, practically underfoot.

I heard the click as someone opened the new padlock on the shed door. The light moved inside the shed.

"What if he don't come?" Rodney asked.

"We go back to your brother's. I ain't going to tangle assholes with Glen, not just the two of us."

Good news there. At least there weren't four on defense and only me on offense, which had been the worst of the possibilities on my mind.

"You got everything on your 'checklist,' Earl?" Making a joke out of checklist.

"Can you believe that shit? Good thing he don't know what's on my checklist."

"What's that?" Rodney said.

"What I got right here in the pocket of my BC. The two extra spears for the gun."

Bad news here. The cousins' original plan had been to try for Glen with a small spear gun powered by CO_2. The trouble with this was that if Earl missed, he wouldn't have time to reload. With me added to the team, though, there was no real use for the gun at all. Rodney and I could handle Glen, with Earl and his spear gun standing by as backup. Suppose, though, that Glen was too much for us after all, and Earl had to shoot him. Who was that second spear for? Well, at least now I knew.

"Got a smoke?" Earl asked.

"Jesus, don't you ever buy none of your own?"

A scratch, and a flare, and then quiet for a while.

"Think we ought to start carrying this shit down?" Rodney said.

"I ain't carrying that cocksucker's gear for him," Earl said. "Bad enough we carried it in here."

"Yeah, fuck him."

The moon had been hidden for a while, and the flashlight would have kept the Thornburghs from getting their night vision. They didn't see me when I got to my feet. Next time the breeze kicked up enough to cover my noise, I moved slow and easy away from my patch of bush. Once I was far enough away so they wouldn't think I had been listening, I called out, "You guys here?"

The light flashed to show me the way to the shed. "Looks like they must be in bed out there," I said. "When did the lights go out?"

"They was out when we come."

"We be able to find it all right with this fog coming in?"

"I took the compass bearing yesterday," Rodney said.

"Rodney can find a lobster pot in the dark, he can sure as shit find a sixty-foot boat."

"Well, let's go then."

Scuba diving is a labor-intensive sport, or it is until you get into the water. It took us twenty minutes of slipping on seaweed-covered rocks to get everything down from the shed to the little cove below it, and then to get all our gear on us or attached to us. At least we were able to use a flashlight to see what we were doing, though. It might have been risky on a better night, but the fog was so heavy that the small light would be invisible from where the *Billene* lay.

"Fog's wicked thick," Earl said. "We could just leave the tanks here and snorkel out, and nobody wouldn't see us."

"We went all through this," I said. "If there's any risk at all that we can avoid, didn't we say let's avoid it?"

"That's just it," Earl said. "There ain't no risk. It's too dark to see, and they're asleep anyway."

"We don't know they're asleep. We don't know the fog won't lift before we get out there, or while we're on board."

"At least we can stay on the surface most of the way," Earl said.

I didn't like it that he was raising questions. Till now my authority in the operation had been beyond question, since I had whipped big Rodney two times running. On the other hand, Earl was right. There was no reason to dive, until we got near the boat. And maybe not even then, if the fog got heavier. Maybe never, if Rodney didn't manage to find the *Billene*.

"Okay, let's stay on top," I said. "But be ready to dive just in case."

I'd much rather have left the tanks behind myself, to tell the truth. The more I had weighing me down, the more awkward and helpless I felt. I was encased in a stifling, binding wet suit, with a bulky buoyancy control vest on top of that, and twenty-five pounds of lead strapped around my middle, and a tube sticking out of my mouth, and a mask giving me tunnel vision, and gloves turning my fingers to sausages, and a hood making it hard to hear, and huge flippers making it practically impossible to walk, and the dead weight of a steel tank trying to pull me over backward. The last time I had felt this confined, this defenseless, was when I was tangled inside a tent in the dark with these same two guys pounding on me.

I tongued the snorkel out of my mouth and said, "Well, fuck it. Let's go."

I felt slightly less clumsy when the water took up most of the weight I was carrying. I had a little negative buoyancy, though, and had to use my fins to stay on the surface until I got more air into my vest. Earl and Rodney were better divers; they had known just how much to inflate their vests before getting in.

Rodney passed the loose end of a buddy rope to Earl, who passed it on to me. The other end was tied around Rodney's waist. The idea was for us to go along behind him, like fish on a stringer. Rodney tugged the rope once—the signals were once to go and twice to stop—and we set out. Rodney was the one who actually had to know what he was doing: judge the time it would take us to come up on the boat, keep an eye almost constantly on the luminous dial of the compass in his diving console, make allowances for tide and currents. All Earl and I had to do was hold on to the rope and keep up.

For the first time I was impressed by Rodney. He just went churning ahead through the water, never hesitating and never hurrying. He was in his element like a walrus or a manatee, doing the one thing he could do really well. Never mind that the patchy fog almost swallowed the moonlight, and that the slight swell made it impossible to see more than a few yards ahead anyway. Rodney churned ahead, and we followed along confidently.

My watch was under the sleeve of my wet suit, and so I didn't know how long we went along like that, in Rodney's wake. But I was starting to feel the strain in my hamstrings from working the flippers up and down. At last the two tugs came. Rodney pushed his mask up onto his forehead and spat out the mouthpiece of his snorkel.

"Should be off to starboard somewhere," he said. After a second I looked to the right. The second was because that's how long it takes me to remember each time that *port* has the same number of letters *left* does, so starboard means right. I didn't see anything to the right, and at first Rodney didn't, either.

"Well, fuck . . ." he said. "Wait a minute, though. See there?"

"I don't see shit," Earl said.

"Over there. Where it's a little darker than the rest."

"Well, maybe."

"We better keep quiet. Come on."

This time Rodney led us very slowly, just barely finning along. Soon I saw the darker bulk, too. Then, when we were just a few yards away, the clouds in front of the moon thinned. Not much light came through, but it was enough for eyes used to the dark. We made our way around to the rear, where a little diving platform made a ledge below the aft deck.

I was the one least at home in the water and most awkward at handling heavy equipment in it. So I was supposed to get rid of my gear and climb on board first. Earl and Rodney helped me off with my weight belt and the buoyancy control vest that my tank was strapped onto. I felt almost light enough to fly. I pulled myself halfway out of the water, as slowly as Glen doing his pull-ups, and rolled myself very carefully on board. The boat was rocking in the slight swell, but Rodney had said that any substantial movement outside of that rhythm might wake a light sleeper. Once aboard, I took off my fins and struggled out of my hood and gloves and wet suit jacket. I spread everything out on the deck. Then I took my weight belt and tank from Rodney and Earl, and set them down noiselessly on the pad made by the wet suit. All this was part of the drill we had gone over and over in Rodney's shed.

Next Rodney and Earl helped each other off with their weight belts, and handed them up. Then the tanks. By the end I had a good-sized pile of gear stacked up beside me. After I helped Earl and Rodney aboard, they fought their way out of their wet suit jackets, too. Rodney was empty-handed. Earl held the miniature spear gun, not much longer than a sawed-off shotgun. It fired a short spear, about eighteen inches long. Normally a coiled nylon cord attached the spear to the gun, so you could haul the fish to you or retrieve the spear in case you missed. Earl had removed the cord. He didn't plan on doing any hauling or retrieving, and the cord would have limited the weapon's range.

"Let me see that thing," I said, holding my hand out.

"What for?"

"I just want to check it. Come on." Before I was finished talking I grabbed it, fast enough so that he didn't have time to tighten his grip on it. I scaled the gun off into the darkness.

"What'd you do that for?" he asked, starting out to shout but remembering just in time to whisper.

"Because you're too scared of this guy. You would have used it on him as soon as you saw him."

"So what?"

"Because I want to talk to him, okay?"

"That's it, I'm getting out of here. I don't want no more parts of this."

"Listen to me, you stupid fuck. You're going to grab that fucking swim fin and you're going to do exactly what you're supposed to do."

I was right in his face when I said this, so he didn't see my move on his wrist till it was too late. I put a wristlock on him and hurt him a little, watching him try not to cry out.

"Okay?"

"Okay, okay."

Earl went for the swim fin while Rodney took his pre-arranged station on the top deck, above the doorway that led out onto the aft deck. I hid on a shelf or ledge that ran along the sides of the boat, a kind of a narrow walkway with a guard railing. Earl, down on the diving platform, started in with the swim fin.

The idea was to make a noise that would need to be looked into, but wouldn't sound threatening. Slapping a swim fin against the side of the boat in time with its natural rolling was what we had come up with. Rodney and Earl figured it would sound as if something had come loose that shouldn't have. That was the theory.

For a long time the theory didn't work. Earl kept slapping, and nothing kept happening. I left my hiding place and tiptoed over to him. "Harder," I whispered. But before he could hit harder, light from a porthole suddenly fell on the water. I just had time to make it back to my station when the door leading out to the deck opened and the beam of a flashlight shot out. The slapping kept up. The beam moved toward it, showing nothing unusual to the man behind the flashlight. Earl and the diving gear were safely out of sight on the diving platform. Glen moved in that direction, and now I could see his silhouette against the light from his flashlight. He wore pajama bottoms but no top. His free hand was empty.

I was behind him, a little off to one side. I stepped out and said, "Hey." Glen whirled on me with the light. Up to Rodney now.

Glen stood still for what would have been a second too long if I had planned to go for him without help. Then he did the sensible thing, which was to run for the doorway he had just come out of. He didn't make it.

Rodney, as instructed, tackled him and hung on. It was the kind of ankle tackle that a good running back can break, but it caught Glen unprepared. He smashed onto the deck hard enough to daze him, and I was on top of him before his brain could organize what was happening. His legs were anchored and helpless and I had the restraining ties around his wrists before he could prevent it. Again our drilling paid off. I had practiced the handcuffing maneuver on Rodney over and over, until it was automatic.

I grabbed the flashlight and held it for Earl while he came over with the buddy line and used it to tie Glen's elbows together behind his back. "Don't pull them so tight together," I said. "You'll cut off the circulation."

"Who gives a fuck?"

"I give a fuck. Not so tight."

By now Glen was tracking again.

"You two," he said, looking at Earl and Rodney, and sounding more pissed off than scared. "Who's this guy with you?"

"Nobody," I said.

"What do you want?"

"Below," I said. "Come on."

13

THE CHEMISTRY OF THE SITU-
ation changed when Billene Somerville came into the
salon, wearing a shorty nightgown barely long enough
to cover her. It was like one of those lab experiments
where you put a drop of red fluid into a test tube of
blue fluid and the whole thing turns some different color
entirely.

"Look what I found, Earl," Rodney was saying. He
had Billene by the upper arms and was pushing her in
front of him like an offering. She was still half-stupid
from sleep, dazed and helpless and not struggling at all.
Billene looked good for her age, or any age. She had fine
legs and the good muscle tone that is the key to a beautiful and durable figure, as women are finally coming to
understand. It's what Brigitte Bardot had and Marilyn
Monroe didn't.

Billene's hair was messy and her face was free of
makeup. She trembled, like a frightened animal Rodney

had caught in his big, solid paws. Like an animal, too, she seemed to have no power of speech. But a powerful appeal came from the way she held herself, from the whole appearance she made. A plea for what, though? Pity? Protection? Love?

"Found something to take along with us," Rodney said to his cousin. "Think it can cook?"

"Bet it can do lots of things," Earl said. "Let's have a look."

Two things happened at once. Earl made just the start of a movement toward Billene, and Glen exploded up from the sofa we had pushed him onto.

With his arms tied behind him, he had to make do with what he had. He charged Earl head down, like a bull, and took him full force in the middle of his narrow chest. Earl went over with Glen on top of him, knees straddling him. None of us was ready for what happened next, probably not even Glen himself. With his mouth wide open, he went for Earl's face like a snake. Earl twisted away just in time, and Glen's teeth clicked on air, loud as a castanet. Earl had his arms up in front of his face now, keeping Glen from him while Glen was making noises like a dog. He was trying to get at Earl's throat, and it took all my strength to pull him off by the loose end of the rope that bound his elbows.

I dragged him to an armchair and tied the free end of his rope to the steering wheel behind the chair. Earl was up on his feet again, full of bravery now that his attacker was tethered. But he didn't get anywhere near the captive, and I didn't blame him. The cording stood out on Glen's shoulder muscles as he strained against the rope, and blood vessels stood out on the cording. He looked entirely capable of tearing the steering column right up out of the deck. Noises were still coming from down in his throat.

And then he mastered himself. You could watch it on his face, the intellect taking back control of the system and jamming the emotions back inside. The rigidity went out of him, the facial muscles relaxed, the cords and ridges in his shoulders smoothed out. His breathing slowed. The flush faded from his skin. An impressive performance, considering he had been a carnivore mad with adrenaline a few seconds before.

Glen's tanned, bald head sat on a thick column of neck. His torso was another solid column, much thicker and braided with muscle. Beautiful bodies don't mean much in wrestling. Guys that look like Apollo are regularly whipped by guys that look like rejects from the jayvee football squad. But Glen wasn't just well built, he was strongly built. There's a difference. If you draw an opponent like Glen, you want to be very careful, even though the guy may not be terribly good. Somebody that strong, all he needs to do is get a little bit lucky, just once.

"What's the rest of your name, Glen?"

"Hofer."

"Where'd you get those tattoos, Hofer?"

"A tattoo parlor."

"Guy did a nice job. What does he do, work in the dark?"

Glen Hofer smiled a pleasant half-smile, appreciating the joke about as much as it was worth. That he could smile at all under the circumstances was pretty good. He was someone to take seriously, but I already knew that.

"What do you guys want, anyway?" he asked.

"Money," I said.

"I guess Mrs. Somerville could arrange that."

"Where is it?"

"Well, let's talk about it a little first."

"Fuck talking," Earl said. "The man asked you where it is."

"Not on board, certainly."

"Bullshit," Earl said. "What did you pay us out of?"

"Oh, the petty cash. Well, sure, that's on board. Is that all you want?"

I decided to let Earl take over for a little while. It would be fun to see the guy tie Earl into knots.

"What else you got?" Earl asked.

"Oh, Mrs. S. has quite a bit in various places, but not on board. She could get hold of some of it for you, I'm sure."

"Yeah, right. While you call the cops. What you got on board? Let's start with that."

"Whatever you see that's worth money. The electronics, I guess. Mrs. S. has some good jewelry in the master stateroom. A mink coat. Just look around."

"Start with the money. Where's the money, shithead?"

"It's a little low right now, this time of month. Look in the galley, the drawer beside the sink. Behind the thing where the silverware is."

Earl came back from his errand in a moment, holding out a leather billfold. "Hundred and eighty bucks? You got more than this around."

"I told you, this time of month."

"Don't try to shit me, or you'll be sorry." He stopped for a second to think of a way to make Glen sorry. Then it came to him and he grinned. "He don't want to give us her money, why don't we take it out of the lady in trade, huh, Rodney?"

Rodney just stood there, slow.

"Take it out in trade, Rodney. Get it? Jesus, just hold on to her for me, will you?" Rodney must have got it; now he was smiling, too. He forced Billene's little hands behind her and held them with one of his while he grabbed a handful of her sun-bleached, bed-tousled hair with the other. She didn't struggle or cry out. She was terrorized beyond struggle and speech. Earl was tugging his way out of the pants of his wet suit. Under it he wore a nylon bathing suit. And you could see that under that, if nowhere else, Earl was an incredible specimen. He pulled the trunks down and it bobbed out, half erect already. It was the kind of thing Long Dong Silver used to wave around in his porno flicks, so big it looked more animal than human. So big, if you could judge by Silver's performances, that it could never harden up properly.

Billene tried to draw back, but Rodney used his grip on her hair to force her face forward toward the thing.

"In the master bedroom," Glen said, his voice under control so tight you knew it was about to break. "There's a platform for shoes on the floor of the closet, kind of a built-in shelf. Safe under it."

"Take a look, okay?" Earl said to me.

"You don't really want to stay here with this guy, do you?" I said. "You go."

This made sense to Earl. A man who had just tried to bite his throat out might be able to bust nylon rope, too. Earl stuffed the grotesque organ back in his trunks and went down the stairs to find the master bedroom.

"It's here," he hollered up after a few minutes. "Get the fucking combination from him."

"Left to twenty-seven," Glen called out, and paused till Earl hollered that he had it. "Right past fifty-three twice and stop the third time ... left past ninety-five once, and stop the second time ... right past ninety once, next time stop at ninety."

"Got it," Earl shouted at last.

In a moment he came back up with his hands full. "I

told you," he said. "Didn't I fucking tell you guys she had more than that around? Take a look at this."

He waved a block of wrapped hundreds at us.

"There's twenty-two thousand down there, how do you like that! Bunch of these things, too."

I took what he held out to me. It was a matured five-thousand-dollar bearer bond, as good as cash and nego-tiable by whoever came up to the window with it.

"Worthless," I said. "These are certificates of deposit. You can't turn them in for another ten years."

"Wouldn't you know it. Fucking safe's fucking full of them."

I caught Glen looking at me. Nothing showed in his face. When he saw me watching, he whispered some-thing I wasn't entirely sure I caught. It might have been, "There's more." I hoped nothing showed in my face either.

"Come on, Earl," Rodney said, bending Billene's head back again. "Give this little bitch what she wants. She's dying for it."

I was going to step in, but not quite yet. I wanted to see what might still fall out of Glen if I let things continue.

This time Earl took his trunks all the way off. He was again bobbing at half-mast, which was no doubt as high as the hydraulics could hoist an object that size. The one who acted really pumped was Rodney. As Earl advanced, Rodney shifted his grip on Billene, so that he could squeeze her cheeks and make her open her mouth. Rodney's own mouth was slack and wet.

All right, enough.

But before I could speak, Billene finally found her voice and screamed to her helpless defender for help.

"Let her alone, Earl," I said, but he was too excited to hear, or to obey. I got to him just before the thing reached her mouth, with a full force slap to the side of the head that knocked him to the floor.

For a few seconds he was too stunned to speak. He looked absurd lying there, a scrawny, naked body with this weird thing in the middle of it, so out of proportion that it looked like something he had strapped on. Earl rubbed the ear I had hit. "What's the matter with you?" he finally managed to say.

"I'm not Rodney, asshole," I said. "Watching you rape women doesn't get me off."

"You fucking hurt me."

"I should have hurt you worse. Maybe I will."

"Jesus, Tom, if you feel that strong about it, go ahead and take firsts."

"Good thinking, Earl. You figured it out why I hit you, huh?"

"Sure, go ahead and help yourself. Pussy don't wear out."

"That's good, too, Earl. Folk wisdom."

"We can keep her around till we get tired of her. We don't have to waste her right away."

"Plan's changed. Nobody gets wasted."

"They got to. They know us."

A thought came to Rodney, for once, before it struck his cousin. "Yeah but, Earl," he said, pointing at me, "they don't know *him*."

This got my attention to Rodney. "Let go of that woman, for Christ's sake," I said. Rodney let go of her right off. I still had the whammy on him.

"Get him, Rodney," Earl shouted from behind me. "He's going to kill us."

He was moving before he finished shouting, heading up the ladder that led to the bridge. I still might have managed to grab hold of his ankle, if Rodney hadn't managed to grab mine. I kicked but couldn't get loose.

He was strong, and I had drilled him too well in how to be an anchor. I had to go for a thumb so he'd let go. He screamed when it broke. Just then Earl reappeared at the top of the stairs, and I remembered too late what he had once said about keeping weapons on the bridge. He had a rifle in his hands pointed straight at me. He pulled the trigger once, twice, before he figured out that the chamber was empty.

While he worked the bolt to chamber a round, I was forcing Rodney to his feet so he would be a shield. Earl and I both finished what we were doing at the same instant, and the gun went off. I felt the shock as the bullet hit Rodney, and heard the breath blow out of him. It sounded like the whoof a deer makes when it jumps from cover. Seeing Rodney hit, Earl just stood there for an instant. And I did the only thing I could.

I went up the stairs for him. I heard the gun go off again, right over my head as I went in low. In a second, operating on automatic pilot, I had him pinned. I pulled the rifle free from under him and tossed it out of reach. Then I got up and looked down at him, lying there naked. If the thought of touching his pride and joy hadn't been so disgusting, I would have dragged him back downstairs by it. I settled for yanking him to his feet by his hair, and kicking him down the steps.

When I followed him down, he was sitting beside Rodney, looking at his cousin in horror. The huge torso was laced with blood, which was still coming out of the hole blown in his chest. It was what the grunts kept talking about during the Vietnam War, a sucking chest wound. I had never seen one where I was, in Laos. The sound was awful, as if something inside his body was gasping and slurping for air at the same time he was gasping himself, through his mouth.

"You stupid fuck," I said to Earl.

And, to Glen Hofer, "Stupid fuck here, where can I lock him up to keep him out of trouble?"

"My cabin," Glen said. "Second on the left down there."

"Any weapons in there?"

"No. That shark rifle is all we've got."

I marched Earl off, not gently, and locked him away. It didn't take a minute, but when I got back Glen had already got Billene Somerville out of her trance. And she was at work on the knots above his elbows. When I showed, she pulled away from him as if she had been caught at something bad.

"Go ahead," I said. "The doctor can't take care of Rodney without his hands."

"The doctor . . ." she said, looking at Glen, and then at me. "Oh my God, how did . . ."

"It's all right, sweetheart," Glen said. "When you screamed for help, you said Denton."

"Oh, sweetheart, I'm sorry. I'm so sorry."

"You couldn't help it. Besides, I would have told him anyway. He's smart, not like that filth over there. I wouldn't be surprised if he already knew."

"I didn't," I said. "And you wouldn't have told me."

"Well, maybe not. We would have had to see how things developed."

"Go ahead and untie him, Mrs. Somerville. Then go put some clothes on."

"Bring up my bag, too, will you, dear?"

When we were alone, except for Rodney sucking and wheezing on the floor, Dr. Somerville said, "There isn't much I can do for him outside of a hospital, you know."

"Just do whatever you can."

He nodded. I looked down at him, sitting in his arm-chair, and considered how he had been able to pull it off. The G. Gordon Liddy mustache to call attention away from the rest of his face. The shaved head for the same reason. I once knew a woman grad student at Harvard who was an activist for the rights of the handicapped, or the otherwise-abled, as people like her said. She had had her head shaved so she could find out how it felt to have the world treat you like a freak. All that I could see of her for a long time was the bald head. It wasn't till I saw her wearing a hat one day that I realized she was beautiful.

And you not only didn't ask too many questions of a man with jailhouse tattoos; you also didn't think of him as a professional man.

But the most effective thing of all was the new body he had built himself. I remembered the slightly paunchy, stoop-shouldered figure in the newspaper photos. The plump cheeks, the swelling jowls. Just an average American male of middle age, which was to say a soft, overweight, unhealthy, weak, and pathetic slob.

Somerville had done the same thing to himself that you do to a house when you tear it down to the framing timbers and start all over again. He stood differently. His head sat on a different neck. He moved differently. His hands were broad and strong instead of wide and pudgy. His shoulders no longer seemed stooped. Now they were slightly sloped and powerful. There was no more resemblance between the new Glen Hofer and the old Denton Somerville than there was between the before and after in those ads showing women who lost half their former body weight.

"You did a nice job on yourself, Somerville," I said.

"I did, didn't I?"

"I suppose P.J. Potter signed your death certificate, didn't he?"

"You know P.J.? Well, of course you do. You must be that, quote, reporter, close quote, who put that idiot

Hostetter in the hospital for six weeks. He lost partial vision in one eye."

"He tripped."

"Really? Then he wasn't lying when he told P.J. what happened. To get back to your question, though, of course you're right. Sure it was P.J. who killed me off. As my physician he kept my charts, naturally, and found appropriate X rays in his old office files to put into my folder. Not that anybody would look, but if they ever did, they'd find radiological evidence of my earlier cardiac episodes as well."

"How about the funeral?"

"One of our companies owned the funeral parlor. P.J. and Billene went down with my gurney to the morgue. P.J. filled out all the paperwork, and saw me wheeled onto the hearse. I saw nothing, of course. Being dead and covered with a sheet."

"Well, it damned near worked, till Billene screwed up."

"Don't tell her that."

"I won't."

"So now you can collect the reward."

"There's no reward offered. You're dead."

"Oh, I think we ought to be able to work out a reward for you."

"Probably those bearer bonds will do. How much is there?"

"A million two. But we can do a little better than that, I'm sure. In fact you might want to be partners with me, working mostly with P.J., of course. You seem to be a pretty useful fellow."

"I'm a pain in the ass, actually. I'm going to turn you in."

"Why?"

"To make myself feel good."

"I could probably make you feel a lot better. Do you have any real idea of how much money we're talking about here?"

"How much?"

"Well, it fluctuates, but P.J. and I have access to funds or control assets worth on the order of four hundred million."

"That's what you slid out from under before the collapse, huh?"

"One way or another, yes. It's pretty complicated."

"Probably the lawyers can sort it out."

"Sort it out and then keep most of it for themselves. That's what would happen, you know."

"I know. Hey, it's a world I never made."

"That doesn't mean you can't live damned well in it."

"There's a couple things here. First off, I already live well enough to suit myself. Second, fucking you over means a lot to me."

"Why? What did I do to you?"

"Nothing. I just like fucking fuckers. You're the kind of slippery, smiling prick that I hate worse than anything in the world. I've known you guys all over the place, Denton. I read about you in the papers every day. You're in the goddamned White House, the banks, the big law firms, the networks, you're every goddamned where. I hate all of you, but you're the particular one I'm going to fuck. Nothing personal. You're just the only one I've got my hands on right at the moment."

Dr. Somerville looked at me as if I had just turned into a koala bear or started to pray in Latin or something. "You mean this is political?" he said. "Some kind of Patty Hearst thing?"

"No, it's just me."

"Good. Then we can work it out."

All this time I had been standing back from him, with

him sitting down. While a man is getting up from a chair, he can't do much for himself, either offensively or defensively. And once Billene came back, which she just then did, I would use her to keep her husband in line.

"Let me see the bag," I said to her. "Hold it open for me."

I found an instrument case with scalpels, and held on to it.

"No problem," the doctor said. "I won't be needing a scalpel."

She handed the bag to him, and he went over to the huge, bloody carcass on the floor. "Bring me towels and some water, darling," he said. "I need to clean him up so I can see what I'm doing."

Billene brought the water, but kept her eyes away from Rodney while she handed it over. Then she went to the galley and turned her back on the whole bloody scene. I didn't. I watched with interest while Dr. Somerville's rubber-gloved hands worked on the mound of torso that went back to its normal paleness as the doctor mopped away the blood. But as fast as he mopped, fresh blood welled up in the hole. The towels turned pink and red. The rubber gloves had smears of red on them. The hair that covered Rodney's belly and chest and shoulders was water-slicked to the white skin. The entry wound had bright red lips, pooched out a little. The escaping air made bubbles in the blood, turning it to froth. Watching, I felt no more pity than I would have felt in a butcher shop, or examining a road kill. It worried me a little that all I felt was interest in what the doctor was doing. The regular sucking noise still came from the wound, and that was interesting, too, while it lasted.

It stopped when Somerville pressed his hand down flat on the yawning wound and sealed it off. "Best I can do without equipment," the doctor said. "But at least now he won't be losing all his oxygen."

"Will he make it?"

"I doubt it. He's very seriously hurt."

The doctor's gloved hand rode the huge barrel of Rodney's chest up and down as the breath went in and out of him. His breath soon began to come fast and short, like a dog panting. And after a while even faster and shorter, as if he were fighting for air that would not come. I thought of my uncle, killed by the American Tobacco Company when I was nine. He had sounded like that in the last months of the years it took for the emphysema to drown him.

Rodney had been quiet when he was first shot, probably in shock. Now he was groaning and crying and trying to sit up with what little strength he had left. Somerville's hand kept him down easily. Rodney's eyes were bulging, and his face got more and more blue. His fat neck grew fatter, swollen like a frog's. The groans of agony went on and on and on, until after an endless time he was released into unconsciousness. The doctor kept his hand on the wound for a minute or so more, and then said, "Damn. We've lost him unless we aspirate fast. Go get the rubber tube out of my bag, will you?"

As soon as I turned away from Dr. Somerville, I heard the noise. I was quick enough to spin back toward him, but not quick enough to avoid his rush. He caught me with my arms at my sides. His hands locked behind my back, and I right away felt the strength that I knew he had, strength that was about to break my ribs. In the instant left to me, I moved my hips back to give myself a little wiggle room, which I used to squeeze his testicles with both hands.

The pain made him let go his grip, so that I could get

a double arm lock above his elbows. I straddled his left leg and dropped back onto the floor, pulling him forward on top of me. I was in a bridge when I hit the floor, and turned him with a whip-over, and did what you need to do in a hurry when somebody that strong wants to kill you. I drove forward, still holding my double arm lock, and broke both his shoulders. Then I got clear of him.

Billene was on the doctor almost before I was off, cradling his head in her lap. Dr. Denton had screamed when the joints in his shoulders cracked. He was still in shock, before the pain came. "Baby, sweetheart," Billene crooned. "It's all right, baby, I'll make it all right. There, there, baby. There, there, sweetheart, darling."

All at once she looked up at me, and screamed, "DO SOMETHING, YOU COCKSUCKER PRICK!"

"Nothing I can do," I said. "Maybe he's got some kind of a shot in there you can give him."

"YOU COCKSUCKER PRICK SHIT, YOU HURT MY BABY!"

As far as I knew, Denton Somerville had never felt sorry for anybody else, so I didn't feel sorry for him. I did feel sorry for Billene; it was impossible not to be moved by her love and her anguish. But I couldn't help thinking that they had picked each other out of a whole world of other available people. It's generally a waste of time to pity people who marry shits and stay married to them. Often enough, the reason they don't notice the stink is because they've got the same smell themselves.

Soon the shock began to wear off, and Somerville's face turned shiny with sweat from the pain. But he looked alert, as if his brain was back in command of the operation. He made a hell of a bad guy, and he would have made a hell of a good guy, too, if he hadn't been

born without that little piece that makes you human—
the piece called pity, or empathy.

"Oh, *shit!*" I said. "There goes that goddamned Earl."

I had just felt the boat rock. It was the sudden lurch
caused when a heavy weight is suddenly lifted from a
platform in balance. A man, for instance. For instance,
Earl—letting himself drop from a porthole.

I ran for the stern.

I couldn't hear him in the water when I got outside.
And I couldn't see him. The fog had thickened so that
visibility was down to almost nothing. I shouted Earl's
name. As I listened, it came to me all of a sudden that
he wouldn't answer and where he would have to be. I
snatched the rifle and headed there myself, down the
couple of steps to the diving platform at the stern where
I had piled our wet suits. Sure enough, when I grabbed
for the pile it seemed to be trying to escape. But then
the resistance disappeared and there was a thrashing in
the water. Earl figured it was better to let go his grip on
the wet suits than to have me catch him.

"Come on back, you dumb shit," I said. "You'll
freeze." All I heard was more splashing, as he put distance between us. I couldn't see him out in the water—
couldn't even see the water. The fog swallowed what
little light came from the boat. "Hey, Earl," I shouted.
"I'm putting the wet suits inside. You want one, come
on back and ask. Incidentally, your cousin Rodney just
died."

I guess I didn't have to pass along that news, strictly
speaking. But boys just wanna have fun.

Back below, I interrupted an argument between Billene and Denton. "Pain doesn't kill you, honey," Denton
was saying. "I've got to be able to think. No sedation."

"Sure, let's think," I said. "What else is on board
except what's in the safe?"

"The boat itself," the doctor said.

"Yeah, that's what those two assholes were after."

"For which they'd have to make sure we were permanently out of the way, I assume?"

"That's what they assumed, anyway. I guess I assume it, too, only I don't want to kill anybody."

"We could sign the boat over to you. There'd be ways to work it out so everybody was happy. We're not in such a bad spot here as you might think, none of us. If we put our minds to it, we can work things out between us. Earl made it easy by shooting Rodney."

"For me he did. Not for you."

"What do you mean?"

Dr. Somerville sounded friendly and curious. It was an amazing performance, given that his arms looked like they were stuck on his body wrong, he had to be in the most intense pain, and he was at the total mercy of a pirate who had just disabled him.

"It's like I told you, Dr. Denton. I want you to hurt. I want you in jail."

"It just doesn't make sense . . . What's your name? Earl called you Tom. Is it really Tom?"

"Tom will do."

"If you're thinking of some Robin Hood kind of thing, Tom, it's like I told you before. The lawyers will just get it. If we can keep them out of it, you'll be rich for life. Not just rich. Big rich. Texas rich."

"No, you'd fuck me out of it. That's what you do. You fuck people out of money."

"You'd dictate the terms, Tom. What other choice do I have? After all, all you have to do is let it be known I'm alive, and I go to jail."

"Which is exactly what's going to happen. Here it is, asshole. I disable the radio, lock up you two, drop the rifle overboard, empty the safe, and take the launch to shore."

"And then?"

"Like you said. Then you go to jail."

Until I got the two of them locked away I had to listen to a good deal more stuff along the lines of whether I wanted to be truly rich. Till the door closed off his voice Somerville kept on doing what he did best: working a mark. What the hell, he might have succeeded if I hadn't known so much about his history. Certainly I had nothing against getting my hands on even more of his money. But Somerville was much better than I was at getting and keeping money. I figured I would never see it, or wouldn't get to enjoy it long if I did. I had E. R. Hostetter in mind, and big, jolly Dr. Potter, with the eyes as flat and cold as stream pebbles.

Lowering the launch wasn't much harder than it had looked through the binoculars from Felicia's bedroom window. The problem was getting the boat ashore in fog so thick that a flashlight showed nothing but its own diffused reflection. The boat was inside a pearl gray cocoon that lit up wherever I aimed the light but left me blinded.

I had taken along Rodney's compass and used it to steer a reciprocal heading from his. That way at least I'd be sure of finding North America, sooner or later. The problem was exactly when. I moved ahead at half-throttle as long as I dared, then slowed down till the propeller was barely burbling at the stern. There wasn't much I could do when I heard the noise of small waves on the coast, since I was already going as slowly as I could manage and couldn't even see as far as the bow. I just kept to my heading until the boat smashed into a rock, pitching me forward, but not far. I had been holding tight to the tiller of the outboard motor, waiting for the crash. I backed off and aimed a little to the right, and crunched again, and went along that way, bumping on and off Islesboro, until the launch finally ground onto something and stuck. It turned out to be rocks covered in seaweed.

I had put my wet suit and boots back on, to keep off the chill. But even with the ribbed rubber boots, I slipped and stumbled on the slick rocks and had to go partway on my hands and knees. It didn't help that I was trying to hold an aluminum suitcase out of the waves, so that more than a million dollars in cash and bearer bonds wouldn't get wet.

I finally made it to dry land.

Still using the compass, I pushed my way through dripping woods till they opened out onto the road. My choices were left and right. I took left, and it was right. A hundred yards or so up the road, my flashlight beam caught the Lamports' mailbox.

I didn't want to sleep for what remained of the night, and couldn't have anyway. I was too worried that I might have messed up somehow, although I couldn't think how. If the Somervilles broke out of their cabin, what could they do in a blinding fog? And if they managed to get ashore and find a phone, what could they do to me then? If they had me picked up, the first thing I'd do would be to tell the authorities who Glen Hofer really was. Even if they got free somehow, their only hope would be for me silently to disappear with the money. So I was home free, wasn't I? Unless there was something I hadn't thought of. So I kept thinking, and worrying.

At seven-thirty I was on board the *Margaret Chase Smith*. The fog had cleared a little, but the foghorn still blared constantly during the crossing. I drove up the ferry ramp and headed south on Route 1, moving slowly until the fog began to burn away. I stopped for breakfast in Rockland, gassed up, and then kept going till I hit the service area near Kennebunk on the Maine Turnpike. By then it was midmorning. I got a handful of change and called the number for the United States district attorney's office in Portland.

Whoever answered wasn't too anxious to put me in touch with a real assistant U.S. district attorney, but she finally agreed when I asked for her name, and told her I knew the whereabouts of a federal fugitive, and told her I guessed I'd have to mail the information in so that the fugitive would have a chance to get away, and naturally in my letter I'd have to mention the name of the person who wouldn't put me through on the phone. She put me on hold.

"Don McClanahan," a voice finally said.

"You're an assistant U.S. attorney?"

"I am."

"Good enough. You ever hear of Denton Somerville? Dr. Denton?"

"The savings and loan guy that died a couple years ago? Sure."

"He's not dead. You got something to write with? I want to be sure you get it right."

"Go ahead."

"Okay, Mr. McClanahan. You tell the FBI or the Coast Guard or whatever, tell them Denton Somerville is on board a motor yacht called the *Billene*. Bill like the name, e,n,e on the end. Billene. Okay? It's anchored in Sabbathday Harbor, in Islesboro. You know Islesboro? Good. Go get him and you'll be on TV."

"I'm afraid that's not the way it works, Mr. . . . what did you say your name was?"

"I don't want my name in this."

"Even worse. I get a call from a guy who won't give me his name, and you expect me to go out to a private yacht with no warrant, no probable cause to get one with, to pick up a dead guy? How am I supposed to do that?"

"That's for you to figure out, Mr. McClanahan. I'm saying he's there, and he is. I'm also saying that my next call is going to be to the office of the Maine attorney general, so I can get a little rivalry going here. After that I call the *Portland Herald*, and next the *Boston Globe*. Well, you see how it'll work. Anyway, that's it, Mr. McClanahan. Somebody's going to get on TV, and if it isn't your boss, I'll be sure to send him a letter tomorrow to tell him I called you first."

"Wait a minute."

"Mr. McClanahan, you got a fifteen-minute head start before I call the Maine attorney general."

I hung up and headed on south, figuring I'd make my next call from Portsmouth. It was an odd feeling to have enough money in the trunk of my old Datsun to keep me for the rest of my life. What if an eighteen-wheeler plowed into me head-on? What about hijackers? Lightning? I hadn't felt this worried about my baggage since I drove my newborn daughter home from the hospital in Fairbanks, Alaska, a long time ago.

14

FOR A WEEK THE TEMPERATURE and the humidity had been in the nineties, August weather in July. Ozone alerts were in effect, and the old folks were dropping like flies. Of course the old folks are always dropping like flies, but the papers only notice when the temperature gets up near a hundred.

Finally last night the heat broke when a cold front moved in from somewhere or other, bringing with it the usual severe thunderstorm activity throughout the region, along with small craft warnings, local flooding, etc., etc. I knew it would happen way before the weatherman. I knew because of old Freddy, who clerked at our neighborhood grocery store back in Port Henry. You'd ask Freddy if it was ever going to cool off, and Freddy would answer, "Always has."

Now that it had, once again, the sky was pale blue and the air seemed weightless. The temperature was about eighty, with a breeze that made it seem cool. Summer days like this, back when I was a kid, I would look out the window at last year's pine needles dancing in the wind that had shaken them off the big tree. The sunlight would catch the needles and make them shine orange-gold against the dark of the woods behind, and I'd think that it was like being inside one of those globes that you shake to make it snow. Then I'd go out and hotwire a car or something. Anyway, it was pretty.

Joey was behind the counter of The Tasty. We had long since got back to being easy with each other again, after the unhappy business of my meeting with the old men. Joey said they had been feeling a lot better about their losses, since Denton Somerville's arrest. The sight of him on TV, being hustled into court by U.S. marshals, had cheered me up, too.

The medical examiner had drawn the obvious conclusion when he saw Rodney lying there with a large-caliber bullet wound in his chest and Earl's prints on the rifle. That ended the matter as far as the state of Maine was concerned, since Earl was beyond prosecution. His body had been dragged to the surface in a lobsterman's line a couple of weeks after Somerville's arrest, maybe nibbled a little by the crabs but no doubt generally in pretty good shape because of the frigid water temperature. Hypothermia would have got him in a matter of minutes as he swam around in circles in the fog. Maybe he finally had sense enough to holler for help, for all I knew. I had wondered about that once or twice when I was down below talking to Dr. Denton, but I didn't wonder enough to go up on deck and listen. If he was too dumb to climb aboard when I had given him the chance, the gene pool was better off without his in it.

"Hey, you know what finally happened on that Dr.

Denton thing?'' Joey Neary said. "Surprised the shit out of me."

"What's that?"

"The old farts are getting their money back."

"What, from the government?"

"I guess. They sent some woman lawyer up from Washington. Jesus, they sent the right one, too, for them guys. Uncle Kevin said she was pretty near as old as him. How late before they retire you down there, anyway?"

"What are you, Joey, some kind of ageist? Remember Ronzo? Those federal jobs, you can stay on till you're a vegetable."

"Yeah? City it's sixty-five, I think. Anyway, this woman lawyer knew just how much each guy took a bath for, apparently. Had Uncle Kevin and them sign a paper that they wouldn't tell anybody but the IRS about it, on account of apparently there isn't enough dough for everybody all over the country so they don't want to piss off the others that didn't get any. Does that sound right?"

"I don't know."

"Sounds crazy to me. Why not spread it around to everybody as far as the money goes, you know? Fucking government. Anyway, Uncle Kevin and them wasn't about to complain. His check showed up in the mailbox yesterday afternoon and this morning he's outside Cambridge Savings fifteen minutes before it opens."

"What was the name of the old woman?" I asked, curious what name she had picked. "The lawyer?"

"Sylvia something. Sounded Vietnamese. It'll come to me. Prath, like that."

"Plath, probably."

"Why, you know her?"

"No, but I don't think Prath is a name."

"Plath don't sound like a name, either."

"I think I heard it somewhere, though."

I heard it maybe once or twice or a hundred times in Felicia Lamport's poetry class. She couldn't stand what she called the nonpoetry of the late Sylvia Plath. Or, as Felicia called her, the non-Sylvia Plath.

"Hey," Joey said. "Look what the cat drug in. You look like shit, Gladys."

It was Gladys Williams, an old young friend who used to be a lab technician for the Cambridge police when I first met her. She didn't look like shit to me, just tired. She looked tired a lot these days, now that she was a medical student at Tufts.

"Thank you for sharing that with the group, Joey," Gladys said. "It helps to know I look as good as I feel."

"Hey, I'm sorry," Joey said, picking up on her tone. "My big mouth."

"Not your fault," Gladys said. "Last night we lost a guy we shouldn't have, that's all."

"What happened?" I asked.

"Seventeen-year-old kid flipped his motorcycle, wound up in a construction site with a reinforcing rod halfway through his chest. The EMT put an occlusive dressing on the wound and didn't know enough to leave a corner loose to let the air out. So naturally the poor kid developed a tension pneumothorax on the way to the hospital. Time he got to the emergency room, it was too late to save him."

"Back up a minute," I said. "Was this a sucking chest wound?"

"It was till that dumb bastard put the dressing on it."

"You're supposed to leave the wound open?"

"Sounds funny, doesn't it? But what happens if you seal the wound completely, the patient's breathing forces air out through the hole in the lung and it can't escape. So a little bit more of it gets trapped in the lung cavity with each breath. Which collapses the lung pretty soon, which means the poor bastard slowly asphyxiates. Must have been awful in that ambulance."

"I can imagine." But of course I didn't have to.

"Jesus, nobody deserves to go that way," Joey said.

"No," I said. "Practically nobody, anyway."